T0147973

Lizi's Wig

— a novel —

Iza Chkadua

Translator – Ia Tsereteli
Proof-reader – Nino Khundzakishvili

authorHOUSE®

AuthorHouse™
1663 Liberty Drive
Bloomington, IN 47403
www.authorhouse.com
Phone: 1-800-839-8640

© 2012 Iza Chkadua. All rights reserved.

No part of this book may be reproduced, stored in a retrieval system, or transmitted by any means without the written permission of the author.

Published by AuthorHouse   5/14/2012

ISBN: 978-1-4685-0489-7 (sc)
ISBN: 978-1-4685-0490-3 (e)

Any people depicted in stock imagery provided by Thinkstock are models, and such images are being used for illustrative purposes only. Certain stock imagery © Thinkstock.

This book is printed on acid-free paper.

Because of the dynamic nature of the Internet, any web addresses or links contained in this book may have changed since publication and may no longer be valid. The views expressed in this work are solely those of the author and do not necessarily reflect the views of the publisher, and the publisher hereby disclaims any responsibility for them.

Contents

Chapter 1

At once after hanging the phone, she put her wig on the head, belted with big iron buckle on her waist and griped her leather jacket. In her haste she dropped her jacket on the stairs, but never looked back, no time for it – she thought and ran to the street like a crazy. She waved the first taxi she saw and told to the driver to go to the outskirt. Before the driver started the car she repeated to him:

-As fast as you can! ... –The driver looked at her, wonderingly, never understood was it a favor or an order... nor was it a girl in his car or a boy. Anyway it didn't matter... nothing at all... And he whirled away with the highest speed. It was a long distance but in ten minutes they were at "Semi's" park. Lizi dropped fifty GEL bonds on a chair. Never waited for change, ran into the park right away. Stepped in, between a group of fighting boys. It took two or three karate tricks to drop everyone down. Some of them were on their back, some of them on prone. Then she turned to her kid brother, hugged him on his shoulders, wiped his bloody cheek with her T-shirt and stopped the first car she saw.

Entering the room sister and brother embraced each other with love. Lizi took off the wig and put it in the drawer. It wasn't first time that she acted this way. Even in case of insignificant noise (or when boys were pushing of pike) she was grasping her wig and ran towards. Without entering in details of situations she was mixed in the heart of mass. Was fighting the culprit (better said, who was stronger than the other) and soon went away from there.

Orphans' parents were perished in Air crash. Their relatives were visiting them at the beginning time to time. They were bringing them lots of food and money. Lizi went to Karate school, started training. Constantly repeating to herself: "I've got to be a great Karateka." As it usually happens soon relatives forgot about them, never called to them, never visited them. Their visits had terminated. Exactly at that time, Lizi started to look for a job. She was asking to everyone:

- If they needed assistant... – finally one lady from her neighborhood took her to her job, in a chocolate factory, near their house, where she had been working for years. First she took her as an assistant then she gave her an independent work. Lizi was sticking labels on chocolate cream jars. She was working so hard that even director of manufactory had heard: "What is it like, were is it heard that the thirteen years old girl works nine hours a day?" They also heard that the girl was orphan. Director of manufactory thought a lot about her. Finally he decided to give an additional salary to a child. So the incapacity of sister and brother was over by the will of generous, kind people, it made them stronger, put them in a habitual life tempo and in very short time made their family a prosperous one.

Lizi bought the wig when she got her first salary. The first salary brought to a child such happiness that she was carrying money in her pocket for almost one week. Then she went to a city central shop... the little girl was standing at a shop window for a long time, was looking at wigs for a long time from outside, she wanted to choose a hair colour, which had also a stylish haircut. As she could not choose and nor buy from outside, now she went inside. First, she took one wig in her hands, had a good look on it and put it back. Then she reached out for another, dark straw were exactly the same as her own hair, put it on her head and looked in the mirror. (And that only because of wonder, how much she looked like a boy). Suddenly she started to laugh. She looked like a boy so much that it surprised her even more. She laughed for a long time and looked herself in the mirror. The shop girl was watching her with surprise. Suddenly she also burst into a laughter..

-That's a boy's wig, young lady! You should see girl's wigs over there –

- No Mrs. I want boy's wig. – answered Lizi and took the money from hip pocket.

The shop girl thought that the girl was buying the boy's wig due to her sport interest. - As you wish – she said smiling at her and wrote her a check. Lizi looked proudly in her eyes, seemed like she festively announced to the shop girl about her future plans... it appeared to her that the shop girl and she understood each other for a moment... But it's hard to figure out in what... understood what... How could the shop girl know, why Lizi was buying the wig. But it didn't matter then, what really mattered was that Lizi made her dream come true... Eventually why had she gone to Karate lessons? Not for nothing she kept the money from her salary for buying the wig... That's it... she thought and went out the store. She went down the way satisfied.

Lizi didn't like (or why would she), when adolescents were fighting and arguing between one another. Cases like that were much often at schools or in streets of the block. Then they were going somewhere to showdown and fight. She was considering herself totally responsible for her little brother. There was no wonder about it, but was it really her business to instruct others how to live? Beat carping boys, or make them to reconcile with one another... Everyone has their own master and had to take care about their kids themselves. But what can one do, when the nature takes its part. When everything depends on heart dictation. Leaving the nature apart, early responsibilities concerning family made her this particular way, care about people and fight for justice was her vocation and a nature.

Once at school such thing has happened: teacher of Russian expelled out of the class a boy mate because of noise. After that she hated Nick and was always mean to him. One day Lizi could not stand it any more and said it right to her face:

- Mrs. Keto! Why do you hate Nick? It's because he's more naughty than others? – Keto turned pale, then she got angry.

- Oh, look at her, she's trying to teach me a lesson or what, shut up you girl! – Never said a word after that, but she had become much merciful to children and especially to Nick.

Since that day Nick and Lizi felt in love with each other. They were sharing the same desk and worshipped upon each other. They even had planned the future plans for a life. Both of them wanted to make an artist career. They even wrote a script, in which they had to play the lovers. By the script Lizi was a doctor, Nick was a badly wounded patient. Their love was beginning this way: Exciting scenes in walls of clinic, long term treatment and Nick's final recovery. The script was ending tragically. Their wedding day was approaching; Lizi suddenly faints, falls in his arms and dies. Nick deposed to her body kills himself. At that part Lizi started crying, shed tears from her eyes and was sobbing. Nick was covering her lips.

- Be quiet Liz! Teacher will hear you... – Then he was frowning himself...

- No Liz, please let's finish it other way... – he was saying.

While Lizi's parents were alive, she was very happy and free.

She was singing, dancing, was walking with her little brother in the streets and telling him the stories before he fell in sleep. Now? Now it's obvious she became another person. She doesn't speak to much, is hard-worker and pragmatic. If she's not at work, she's out in a gym. Or at a shopping, or is taking care of her brother at home.

Her boyfriend Nick was visiting her very often, was sitting next to her, spoke to her for a while. But Lizi didn't care for private life any more. Neither she wanted love, nor Nick's visits. Family drama happened to be stronger than love. Before leaving Nick was foisting money in Lasha's hands (secretly for Lizy) and whispering him in the ear:

- If you'll need something just call me man! – Lasha was refusing, didn't want to take money but Nick was insisting. Nick was taping him on the shoulder like a man and saying to him:

- What's wrong brother, you'll return it back when you'll grow up. – And was leaving them in a harry.

When the time passes, Nick changed his way too. He forgot love too and mixed up with careless street boys. First he tried alcohol drinks then drugs. Finally! At last odious to himself by senselessness, he disappeared from Lizi's life at all.

Chapter 2

Time has passed quickly. Lasha was fourteen and Lizi twenty two. Lasha was interested in Photography. If he's not in the street he's out there somewhere with his camera. He shots everything, is it a tree or a bush, is it mountain or suddenly noticed person in the street, who's a bit different from others. He has a large collection of pictures. But he doesn't have Lizi's photo. Lizi doesn't like to take pictures, therefore Lasha was taking her pictures secretly. In a hurry by pushing the button and then running away. On sound of the camera Lizi turns to him and runs after him from room to room. Lasha deletes the picture from the camera and looks very dissatisfied. Lizi holds him and tells him that she doesn't like to take pictures.

-You've got to understand me Lash!... I don't like to take pictures – and some how they reconciled at last.

Lasha has her photo anyway. The only photo, that Lizi doesn't know. Bounded in a thin blanket holding sports magazine in her hand and sleeps. Only a professional photographer can take such a picture. In that magazines there is an article about her, when she won Karate contest in spring, magazines and newspapers were overstocked by her pictures. Lizi can't help that contest, the winner will be at magazine covers anyway. Also that's different, Lizi's another person there, she's a sportsman and a winner. That's why it doesn't bother her, on the contrary she likes it.

Lasha is already a big boy. He's grown up and there is no wonder that he goes out to the street often. He communes and argues with boys. Lizi watches them through the window, later, (as if accidentally) she goes to the boys and starts to speak with them friendly. If she can't get to them her point, she mercies none of them. She'll give them in the neck one or two and everything ends beautifully

In the block they call her "Karateka". She weights more than middle... tall, straightened, walks fast with sportsman step. Straw-coloured hair (her hair doesn't need to be combed) simply put her hair up in a bullet bun (It's obvious when she doesn't wear wig). Right refined cast of features seemed nicer this way. (But she wasn't doing it for beauty, doesn't even know about that, it's just more comfortable for her).

Lizi never remembers that she's a girl and a little spruce up wouldn't be bad. It's not to speak of accessories. Never even looked at them. Never had a dress on and never loved none (after Nick), hadn't been in love. She's so used to sport and boy life style, she even doesn't think that she'll ever live woman's life. What ever she does she does it for her brother's sake, the reflex of defending him is so strong that she always tells him the same:

- Tell me when you are going with the boys to fight, don't hide anything from me. - Lasha doesn't say anything, well how can he say anything, this underlines his weakness and cowardice. He's not a little boy any more... Lizi doesn't realize that it's too much, that Lasha is in a process to become a man and now he wants to defend himself and his beloved sister by himself. In her way Lizi's right too. She's been raising him for nine years like a son. Can't help habitual care, how can she stand without controlling little brother. It's not easy to make such a sudden change in her life... tear oneself from the diurnal monotonous rhythm and begin other, unusual life. Inattentive access to, what calls essential object control... and Lizi doesn't understand him.

When she graduated from Physical Culture she became more consequent. (Well she was consequent before), she was doing everything consequently, by results of perpetual training and desire she became Karate coach. Had a good salary and served to her favorite labor.

It the morning Lizi has a habit to get up at seven o'clock. She does gym for half an hour, than she takes a shower and after fixing some breakfast starts waking up Lasha. She never had broken this tradition over the years. It was hard for Lasha to get up early but there is no choice.

- You can't miss school – Lizi used to say. This phrase is so much set in Lashas brain that even when he sleeps he can here it. Lizi also calls him "sleepyhead" and in such calls Lasha wakes up. Drinks tea very quickly and runs to school. Lizi goes to window and watches the little brother before he hides behind the buildings. Mother used to follow her with her eyes when she was running to school and prayed for her.

Chapter 3

Nick was walking with his head hanged and only one thought was whirling his head ... where is my place? Where my destiny calls me... Where can I run away from all this... that is torturing and tormenting me this way... He stood on pavement for a moment, as if he was looking for someone he looked back, looked at the sky, than he turned back. Suddenly he crossed the street with anger. He haven't got anything against people nor to God. He was against himself against his own unconformable existence. That he couldn't fit in this existence no way, nor to himself and it was greatest unexplained suffer to him.

If you would ask him what he wanted from humanity he wouldn't know an answer. He wished something he never even realized... what he never tasted yet never felt yet. Something new. Not money, not glory he had enough all of this and he was enough of it, he wants something unusual, what never really had existed. Is not designated by nature nor is made artificially.

- Any way life is too senseless, monotonous and uninteresting – It was his word and it was his pain.

First he thought, that love, expectation of great and inimitable sensation was the reason of his eternal search, what he had once in a school period, when he was madly in love with Lizi. Than he met mass of girls, it seemed like he was in love with them or may be not... Lika, Teo, Eka... But Tika, oh, yes she... she was different. I really loved her... concluded he, but then he hit the skits and proceeded his way. He remembered that he had hurt her and couldn't show up there any more. Suddenly he stopped, seemed like he remembered something, he looked at the sky. May be it's not normal to look for something what doesn't exists in the world, and never had taken the place in anybody's life...

When he couldn't realize what he really needed, why was he so exhausted to anything, he decided to do something new... No matter what, but extraordinary, something never seen never felt by him before. He rose up to garret, walked there for a while, he even sat down, finally he thought what he was doing there, what was he looking for and quickly got down.

As he entered the room he went to book shelve, first he took one book then another. Read one or two indents and closed them at once. "Why is everything so uninteresting and boring" he thought once again and went out to the street.

He saw old couple in the street. They went out from the store and followed down the road:

- What makes them happy – he laughed for himself ironically and turned his back on them, opposite he saw young man, who was holding the hand of a little boy. The little boy was holding a new box with toy car in it and was looking at father with a happy smile.

- Everybody's happy about something, everybody's got its own way found, what's wrong with me? ... Then he kneeled right on pavement. He remembered his father's words:

-Nick! Son! a man without his business is sad and poor. Never stay out of action...

Nick's parents were raising him in luxury, but his father was always telling him:

- Nick! Son! a man should always have a business, never forget that. – Then it was words spoken on foreign language to him, which he couldn't understand. He didn't understand it because he doesn't find them interesting nor suggestive... That's why he never listened to them. He thought the life would always be like this. He would always have parents and every vital problem would be resolved by itself... Now the time arrived for him to perceive little by little the idea and the meaning of those words. Sadness pushed him to think over. He's been around almost the whole Europe, he lived everywhere. Then he went to villages most beyond, hoping to find there something new and interesting, but watching the poor people and traditional habits almost had drowned him in madness and he ran away from there too.

Finally, he locked himself in the house. All the days walked up and down in the room. He was asking himself what he was looking for, what he wanted. He was asking himself what forces made him to be in eternal searching, why he couldn't find a peace... Finally he sat down and wrote:

"God! Where are you... do you here me?... I can't stand it any more... sat me free... I'm enough of it all... let me find myself... my place... I want something what I've never have seen before... never have felt before. Let it be what ever, but new."

He felt some kind of relief. He folded the paper and put it efficiently in the drawer. He lay down and slept at once. It would be midnight when he started to toss. Toss was followed by delirium, he was dashing around in sleep, moaning so sorrowfully, one would think that his body was burning at fire and he was trying to put it out, at the same time he was desperately calling something, seemed like he was viewing a bad dream. He stood in such situation for a long time, then he jumped up to his feet, watched around, you would think he was looking for someone. Suddenly he tumbled into the sofa, such an alleviation and peace were on his face, he didn't look like himself at all. He seemed to find a way out, found what he was looking for such a long time.

Next day he got up early. He went to swimming pool. He hadn't been there for months, he stood there for a while, then he visited a small snack bar, fended off the hunger. When he entered the house he didn't want to rest any more. He turned on the TV and lay on the bed. He learnt from TV that it was the Fifteenth of April. Georgians were celebrating Loves Day today.

Nick! Nick!! – Koka's voice sobered him down.

He looked from his terrace. There was BMW in the yard.

Come on, get down! – Gaga was waving to him. – Hurry up we are going to Mtskheta.

I'm not coming, you go! – he said without enthusiasm and entered the house.

The boys were taken aback, first they were surprised then they were offended.

Leave him alone, don't you know, he doesn't feel and act very well for last time – Zura said and broke away the car. Nick breathed with relief when he heard the car had gone.

He lifted to the garret and opened the box. Opened the paper list and read it. What a sadden fulfillment of the written letter, petition to God... At the same night... What a mysterious thing life is... man can never reach it's point. He discovered another man in himself, seemed like he was born once again and a new person arrived into this world.

What is wrong with him, everything makes him happy, everything is pleasant to him... what was bothering him two days ago? What did he want? What was he looking for? The essential problem was in him, in him and nowhere else.

The telephone ranged, he took the mobile sluggishly from the pocket and looked "who can it be" – thought he and answered with a changed voice. It was Lasha, Lizi's brother. I'll see you at once – he said and pointed him a date time. Three days later he gave to Lasha some packet – don't tell to anyone, don't mention anything to Lizi – he warned him and went away.

He phoned Tika and asked her to let him see her. At first Tika was surprised, then she told him to come. Nick crossed himself on a crossroad. Hooked up the jeans jacket and entered in a flower store. He'd been there many times and he'd been recognized. Shop girl gave him beautiful bunch of starlings; she knew Nick was always buying these flowers for Tika.

I want us to lift to Djvari, didn't say any more word. Tika was ready in five minutes. They stopped taxi at a Djvari rise.

- Lets walk ok? – It was Nick's wish. Tika agreed without any word. She was very surprised by Nick's behavior. She didn't know this kind of Nick. She was surprised, but couldn't say a word. Monastery was almost empty, they made a circle around the monastery walking with holding hand in hand, than they got down the slope. Finally Nick started to speak.

- I swear to God Tika! I love you very much! I'll never touch drugs, never drink alcohol, never betray you I swear. – Tika didn't believe it of course, but told him that she did. Nick was pleased with her answer.

...This is new also, he had never heard that someone did believe him... No I will never change my mind. Doesn't meter... will it be me or Nikoloz, me or Zurab, or Aleksandre... I will be instead of everybody... only me... because I'm the one who kills everything... useless wishes, evil lust, pernicious habits... Tika broke the silence:

- I do believe you Nick!... You're so different! Before you was fighting all the time... You were confusing us: Lika, Teo, Natia, me... now you don't, you call me my name. You're really different I swear!...-

After some time she added:

Will you be always like this Nick? Tell me Nick!... –

Nick was nodding her and smiling, he was happy about everything.

As he returned back he tidied up the room. He threw away cigar butts. When the sun rays that gamboled through the window (that's

11

how he saw it) made him very happy. In the evening he phoned his old job director if he had something for him. Anything, he just wanted to work – The director repeated the same question for five times:

Nick! Is that you? – He just couldn't believe that it was the same idler and spoilt boy talking to him. Amazed dated him at the work.

Nick started to work at motor assembly factory, he felt that it was new and interesting to him. He was glad about everything. He was glad that he was doing something that someone was satisfied with him and someone needed him... But sometimes he was sad anyway, sometimes he was finding a place to stay alone and was walking thoughtful. He couldn't help the nightmare of that night... When he was coming back to consciousness, he was getting back to work. Directors were very surprised of this transformation, his diligent work. Before when his father brought him to the factory he never did anything, he was arriving late, and leaving early. Now he's accurately diligent, has a good behavior. He acts well with the people whom he has hurt before, he was doing his best to make them feel good.

But the most important thing was that he reconciled Tika. He visited the toy store when he got his first salary and bought the same toy car, which he saw at the street in hands of baby boy with his father. He was carrying it like something incredibly precious, like hope and salvation, like a symbol of victory above the unpleasant past.

He suddenly ran into Lizi accidentally, Nick stood in front of her and told her modestly:

Excuse me Lizi. Our dreams had been broken. We never finished our screeen nor could play our roles in a film. Love passed away too... – He could hardly talk with his head dropped lower:

You was always interceding for me, fighting, do you remember how we loved each other... finally I understood you didn't loved me any more. I went away from you and it was my biggest mistake... You are the best girl in the world, whom I know. – Suddenly he wanted to open his heart to her and as to most close person to him, like in a childhood, he told her his big secret:

- You know Lizi I saw the hell. In my dream... Yeah the hell... It turned me to conscience Lizi... Wow it was something... – Lizi smiled and then looked at the toy. She asked with a surprise:

- Have you got married Nick? Do you have a child?... You got wise?... – Now she held her friend sincerely. Held him and also said good bay to him.

It was obvious he didn't have a child yet. But an expectation of him arriving and this small toy was bringing the joy to his heart.

Chapter 4

After three months holidays new school year has begun. This is the very special day. It's true that Lasha still caries an old bag and he's a little bit sad but so what?... His sister has found a new well paid job so she'll buy him what ever he wants. A new bag and all the other school stuff. What is most important, he will go to football school. He'll buy a uniform and the ball. He's dying for having an uniform number 10. It's the same number that Georgian "Dynamo's" football player Davit Kipiani was appearing on the field. This player was the one whose play made Lasha to fall in love with football. Really! there's nothing like a sport, not sport in general but in particular the football. Absorbed in thoughts, his class teacher brought him to sense. She has patted him on the head with a motherhood care and led him into the class.

As he went out of the school his classmate boy has rushed near by, put his head out of the car window and showed him an expensive "Adidas" ball. The boy was shining with happy smile, it was obvious his father has rewarded him for "good playing", Ladi had been studying football since he was a little boy and he's a good player. Suddenly his father turned his way, told him to get off the window and the father and son had passed by walking boy riding a last model of brand new "Mercedes".

Lasha's heart was broken. He used to had a father too, rich and authoritative. He also had a care from his parents, about whom misfortunately he knows only by stories, he may be also was happy and careless when he was a little boy. But... where are they now, and where is the happiness... Hung his head and walked on. What a misfortune... he doesn't have nor mother not father. Kakhaber for example doesn't have a father but he has his mother alive so he doesn't feel the orphanage so much. But for Lasha Lizi is mother and father, but now Lizi doesn't know that her beloved brother is so much attracted by football, that Lasha's only desire is to run over the field, make some goals, not some, but lots of goals and to become a great football player... How many times has he tried to ask her to take him to football club, but for some reason he couldn't dear. Eh... Hung his head and walked on his way. At the corner of the street Lizi ran into him.

- Borther, have you come?.. she hugged and patted him. – I am in hurry to training, have a dinner and do homework...- she told quickly and went away. Lasha followed an eye to quickly walking Lizi, smiled constrainedly and walked on his way. "I wonder why she can't see that I wish to train myself too... That I wish to practice football too... But how can she see that... She's not a boy... For her it's principal for me to have books, to study languages, to be dressed clean and nice. Why am I blaming her? I have never told her about this... Lizi loves me very much I also know she does everything just for me. When she has found out that I'm obsessed with photography she bought the best camera for me. She gave a lot of money in one, she never even thought twice about it..."

Lasha dropped his bag on the chair, turned on the TV and sat down. "Here it is football again... I wonder who's playing"... Suddenly irritated Lasha turned off the TV and went to the computer. He has recently signed in Facebook, it's a good site, but there's too much gossip. Why do I have to know which opposite party has given a kick to the government, or who's sending his military troops to Iraq. Lasha risen, turned off the computer too and enter the room. He took his camera and went out.

There is a park in twenty meters of the house. There are huge linden and pine trees in the line. This year town leaders had arranged to plant beautiful flowers in the middle of the park, exactly where the little waterfall falls beautifully, it's a wonderful view, it's hot and it drops its spatters pleasantly. Suddenly he saw a little girl, who was wearing multicoloured sunglasses and was eager to get to the waterfall. Lasha smiled, prepared to take a picture. The girl started to run around the garden, she was pleased by boy's attention. She was running from the one place to the other and waving the boy and giving him a sign to take her picture. Father was reproving the child, but it doesn't make her calm, she was laughing lovely and playing pranks. Suddenly she ran to Lasha, hold his hand and brought him to dancing clowns, stood coquettishly and asked him to take a picture of her right here. Father reproved playful Ani and took her to the exit. Ani started to cry and began to watch behind. She was waving to the boy. Lasha got merry by the little lovely girl. He sat down on a branch nearby and got lost in his thoughts.

He doesn't have any friend called intimate. "But the soul needs it most of all someone who's always there, someone who'll always understand." He's a little bit more close to Dato. He's most open hearted with him. He's a bit different than the others. Therewith he lives nearby. Let's visit him... he said and rose up.

Dato was glad to see him, took him in to the room. He was desperately in love and the only thing he wished to talk about was Nia. He was telling him about yesterday events for a long time. How he brought the girl home and how hard it was for him to say good bye to her. Lasha stood quiet. He never said a word. He has other problem in his heart. Something else was bothering him, something obscure and strange for Dato. Suddenly he stood up.

- Where do you run to... stay please... – Asked the boy. Lasha stopped looking him into his eyes and suddenly asked:
Do you steel practice football? –
- Yes buddy! Of course... You know I can never give up football – His face shined with a happy smile. Lasha wanted to say something else, but he held himself back, neither with Dato he can be open hearted... He also couldn't understand anything of him...
-OK I'll go – He said and quickly said good bye. He was on such a mood that spite was filling his heart... What is wrong with this football. Why can't he tell it to his sister. He was walking as fast as he could, he heard foot steps. Dato was running after him, he stood right in front of him breathing hastily.

Tell me Lash! why did you ask? –
Just for nothing – the boy shrugged his shoulders.
No, not for nothing... It seems like you need something – Lasha stood quiet.
Tell me Lash please... Say it buddy... – Do you want anything? –
Nothing –
Nothing at all? –
No –

OK – Dato turned away, but he was quit sure now, he decided something.

Saturday morning, at nine o'clock Dato stopped in front of Lasha's house, stood on his toes and called him out of the window.
- I have a match today, come please come with me –the boy asked with supplication. Lasha's face shined. He quickly dressed up in a sports wear and walked outside. They walked silently. In couple of minutes they were on a field. Players had started the game. Dato mixed with them too. Lasha sat down nearby and started to watch. In the middle of the game Dato approached to the coach and whispered him something in his ear. The coach looked at Lasha, viewed him for a while than he gave him a sign to come by. Lasha was confused, stood up and walked towards the field heavily. The coach shook his hand as an old buddy, asked him few questions about himself, finally told him to "enter the field" and blew the lip whistle.

Lasha entered the field with the wings on his back. The passion that has grown for all these years has become reality. So unexpectedly Lasha found himself in the middle of the field, he dreamed about all his life. Dato as if from the suddenness noted the surprise on his face, "it's good that you're here" - he said and gave him a pass. The boy was running on the field as if he had been doing it for all his life. In just two minutes he made a goal. It was obvious the coach liked the boy. He took him apart after the game and spoke to him, he told him not to miss training and said good bye. Lasha wasn't walking, he was flying home. Not less happy Dato was looking at him time to time slowly and was smiling for himself.

Lasha's life had radically changed so suddenly and unexpectedly. At the daytime he was on trainings and at night he was studying his lessons. Lizi didn't know anything for a long time, Lasha hadn't courage to tell her and was a little worried because of this, but in just ten days Lizi came to know everything. She sat down near her brother and started to speak with him:
Do you practice the football boy? – Lasha nodded to her.
Why didn't you tell me, didn't you need a ball and a uniform?.. – I have got ones Dato gave them to me. –
- Give it back to him, I'll buy them for you, why did you hide it from me? Have you thought I would be furious? – Lizi held his

little brother nurtured by her as a son and started to cry. Lasha held her too looked her in the eyes and asked her with disturb:

Why are you crying Liz? –

Just for nothing, I have recalled mother – Lizi shook her tears.

- Tomorrow we will go to the sports store together. I will buy a brand new ball for you. - Lizi jumped up quickly and left the room. Lasha's happiness was overwhelming. Because Lizi knows she'll give to all this some special perfection. Lizi will do anything to make her little brother happy... That night, the boy slept by the most serene sleep in all his life.

After returning home from school he was running to practice football. He has a training almost every day. Coach liked the boy very much and predicted him a great future.

Chapter 5

Lizi made a big surprise to returned Lasha from school, long wished "laptop" was bought by Lizi, personal computer only for him and said to him:

You'll study well, You'll learn English and you'll practice football as well. You'll go outside seldom. Did you get the point little brother?, – She caressed him and put big plate of meat course in front of him. Lasha was so happy he didn't want to eat anything he was eager to turn on the computer, but he couldn't disappoint his sister and swallowed few bites. Then Lizi took him in his room and opened the laptop on the table.

I'm going to the swimming pool. Don't forget your English lesson. I love you little brother – Held him and left the house quickly.

Lizi really could save him from lot of troubles from the awkward age boys. Boys in a stage of person formation and self-affirmation did not wish to listen to no one. Lasha couldn't find a way to get away from his sister's constant control. He was telling her that he's no longer a little boy and she should live him alone but all was no use. When he was a little, Lizi had a mother-son's instincts so she didn't want to hear anything from the brother.

- Don't fight with each other... stay at home... study a lot... – was she leaving a word and going out.

It was warm spring day. Lasha was talking to boys in the street through his window. People were spread in the streets. Boys were joking, were watching the passengers and endowed them with different calls on their language... Suddenly some boy showed up on the street, he was crying loudly:

- Posters! famous people's posters... Who want famous people's posters – and was showing posters to everyone, some of them he was holding next to his chest. Boys started to laugh at him.
- Common, show them to us?- As if they would buy them, brought him near. Took their posters away from him, then one of the boys told him ironically:
- So you like Angelina boy? –
- This one must be your wife, mustn't she? – Achiko pointed to Nikole Kidman's poster... Lasha asked:
- Leave him alone boys, he is so pitifully dressed... – he pointed at old trousers and jacket... – He has tasted orphanage too so he interceded with him.

If you are so sorry for him, buy him then, your sister has money coming out of her years, she's got a job since she's five... – Suddenly boys made a loud fun of it.

It was a last straw of anger for Lasha.

Leave my sister alone you bastard, how dare you... –

If you're such a macho don't cry from the window meet us at "Semi's" park at five o'clock. There we will tell you the rest... they dated him at park for fight.

I'll be there, wait, let's go right now – said Lasha and never even looked back.

Quickly ran down the stairs. He still can't figure out who made a phone call to Lizi. All was done as it was wanted. One week later boys recognized their guilt, and kept themselves far from Lasha, they were controlling themselves as soon as they were seeing Lasha from far away.

After they had finished taking the shower sister and brother had a light dinner. Lasha made himself comfortable next to computer, Lizi went to give a watermelon to neighbour lady. Granny Nina lost her son last year, since that Lizi takes pity on her. She was often buying her sweets too with her salary. Lizi was a little girl when granny Nina was friend of her mother. She didn't like appearance of this woman because then mother paid all attention to her and Lizi felt all alone then. When ever the door was ringing Lizi was sharping her ears tremblingly and telling her mother:

- It's that nasty lady again... – Mother was covering her lips with her fingers and asking her to be quiet so nasty lady would not hear what she said and was going to open the door.

Now granny Nina doesn't have anybody except Lizi. Lizi specialized geriatrics, thanks to granny Nina. If granny Nina faints - Lizi's here, had a headache – Lizi's her doctor and cares.

In the morning, when she already did the breakfast the telephone ranged, it was Ana. Lizi shouted from happiness:

- Ani! How are you? how's Tika?...

- What?... Are you coming? Wow! That's great?... We'll wait for you, yes we're at home dear! Hurry up then... As she hang up the receiver and crossed Lasha's way from the bath with sparkles in her eyes:

- Well guess who's coming?

- Ani and Tika? – Lasha could read on Lizi's face the reason of her happiness...

- Yes, dear! They'll be here in fifteen minutes. Let's go to market, and make "Meetana" cake surprise for girls.

They went out at once and ran down the stairs with their arms round each other in an embrace with ringing laugh. In a few minutes they hardly were lifting up the stairs loaded by food and provisions.

Liza and Lasha had an aunt in other town, which has lost her husband when she was young and raised two girls all by herself. They were very loving girls, they loved everybody, and specially their cousins that they were eager to come to town every day. They were visiting them once every two months.

When sisters stepped out of the train Ani suggested to catch a taxi as she was much tired. Tika dropped a wild look at her:

Have you forgotten young lady that we don't have more money than to visit a doctor and than go back home? – She said.

All right, don't shout at me – Said sadly Ani.

Wait, where is the bag that mother gave us? – Tika started to look around.

Oh, we've left it on the train... – Tika suddenly realized the case. She turned back and ran quickly; she wildly pushed the conductor at the train stairs.

What's wrong girl, you just went out, didn't you? –The conductor asked.

Well I have forgotten my bag, you know, my bag... – Answered she quite rudely and entered the carriage.

When she turned back, she dropped at the conductor the same wild look, as making her understand that it's not her business where she will go and then she ran back to Ani. The train conductor had shrugged her shoulders, - who is that - mumbled she and got back to her job.

Chapter 6

Stretch, little, serpentine road, submerged in a greenness. Tall spruce and pine trees were spraying the strangest smell all over. The road was going upper and upper. No one knew where the end of the road was, because no one ever had tried to go to the end of it, there was no need in it and no one ever had been possessed with a desire to go that high. This rise was exactly where they lived. A woman with two daughters. When Ani started to have heart problems all the doctors recommended them to move into town. Very soon they moved to table land. In a little town, there were two hospitals and three schools. But soon the girl got respiratory failure again, her heart was beating strangely, the doctor was listening to her heart it was making a noise of a toy spring. Doctors were discussing, consulting. Finely, they advised her to make an examination in a specialized clinic of the capital.

Ana and Tika understood each other when they were in the tenth class. Before that they were always quarreling, were spending their time in arguing and disputing. Ani was two years younger then her sister. They had very different characters. You wouldn't say they were raised in one family, not even on one planet. Elder sister was very singular person... with distinct point of views and also poseur. She was spending most of her time in front of the mirror and every day was changing various dresses. Was it brooches or earrings, beads or something else, she was wearing everything at the same time on her chest and hands. Lizi gave her all the adornments of her mother considering that she's such a poseur. Tika was so happy then that held Lizi and kissed her and told her 'love you' for thousand times.

Little sister Ani was good companion and too communicative that's why neighbours and friends loved her very much. She is also very inquisitive and a tiny wise woman.

Two years ago they had noticed that she was loosing a colour, got tired very soon, hardly breathed and that's why they had visited the doctor.

Tika was leaving the school when she opened her little secrete to her little sister. She wanted to share with somebody that she liked a classmate boy. She liked him or loved him she wasn't sure. She had read large introduction monolog to Ani before telling her this. She started by saying that young lady can be attended by love some day, what should not be a reason for no one to censure her. Ani was nodding to her in a proof of agreement. When it was clear that she could be understood and even more to compassionate her she widely told her short love story. That she was in love with her classmate boy who was sitting backwards, and she was madly in love with him. Since that day they became friends. They became real spiritual sisters. Ani understood her as no one could in the world. Tika was happy she was telling her with great interest even a very insignificant things because she new her sister would understand it, that's why.

After that they became inseparable bodies, couldn't live without each other. They were searching for each other all the time, but as it often happens one is always stronger than another. Ani was physically weak. Tika was strong. When Tika was seeing that Ani's in trouble, Tika could become a salvage animal, there was no obstacle or fair, she could overcome everything, just to see Ani peacefully and safely.

Chapter 7

The time was too lengthened out for Lasha. He called his sisters in low three times on the cell phone. – Aren't you coming, are you coming or not- ... When the doorbell rang, sister and brother ran to the door at the same time... all of them held one another... they were speaking evasively from the happiness they felt. Finally, Tika took Lizi to separate room and whispered her that Ani had a heart weakness, respiratory failure and that's why the doctors sent them away from their own town, they wanted her to be examined in best clinics properly. Lizi was shocked with this unexpected news, but she reassured Tika anyway:

We will arrange everything for tomorrow. – In the morning, before visit the clinic Ani had such a terrible attack that Lasha was terrified.

What's wrong with Ani, dear sister? –he was asking to Lizi.

Doctors will tell. – Was Lizi's answer.

Ani's diagnose was severe form of heart disease.

- Operation is urgent and inevitable –The doctor said. Tika and Lizi cried a lot at the hospital hall. Ani had been told that she's going to need a little micro – operation. There was another problem. Heart operation was very expensive, where could they get so much money. Even if they would sell everything, it wouldn't collect that much. What can they do, where can they go? Can't figure out anything and just stare at each other with a sorrow.

When Lasha realized the situation he asked how much money they needed for an operation... when he got an answer, he just whistled once and knitted the brows. Since that day he was always out. Lizi's intuition was telling her that Lasha was up to something. He seemed changed a lot, acting different. She got scared for him not to commit any kind of crime. When she could get alone with him for a moment she was always mentioning that she could get a credit from the bank in terms of her job certificate and would be able to pay Ana's operation. Everything will be all right, and she was giving him a forced smile.

A week later at three a.m. Lasha put the pack of dollars on the table, called his sister and told her:

- Count it Lizi. – Lizi was shocked.

- What is it Lasha? Where did you get that? – The angry tone was noticed in sister's voice.

- My friends gave it to me. Will it be enough for the operation?

- It's a lot of money, where did you get it. Where... explain to me right now... Lizi seemed to be in sane.

Lasha was sitting quietly.

Give it back, right now – Lizi shouted.

Don't worry, there's no need to be worried. Just count it ...

So you say nothing's to be worry. Who gave you so much money. Tell me at once. – Shouted Lizi more.

Don't shout sister, I will not return anything, it's impossible...

We don't need this I'll save up the money myself... – Lizi was trying to

persuade her brother. Lasha was shaking his head it was shown on his face that he never would give back the money.

Lizi had a fit of hysterics. Lasha watched her face excited as he had never heard her shouting. He was looking at her with astonishment. Lizi had never shouted to his brother before. This unpleasant suddenness lighted the sparkles through his eyes, soon they became in tears and felt down his cheek, but couldn't say a word. You could hear sister and brother fighting quite a long time. Ani's head showed up from the next room's doorway.

What's wrong? – She asked with a sleepy voice.

Nothing darling. Go back to bad – Lizi griped the money and hid it behind her back. These fight and argue took them a lot of time, finally Lizi took him to the door and said to him:

Let's go right now both of us and let's give back the money, at once. Lasha objected, freed his hand from hers and looked at her angrily. At that moment Lizi lost her temper, got closer to him and slap him in the face. It was very unexpected for Lasha. He looked at her with dilated eyes. Lizi suddenly felt that it was no longer his brother's look, some stranger was looking at her, and she regretted what she did at once, but this couldn't help the situation... He was so far from Lizi right now, that she totally forgot that she was patron of this family and of her brother. She looked like a bondwoman. She became an unpaved

25

woman. Lasha turned his back on her. He ran away dumbfounded to his room and locked the door. He was sitting dressed on the bad till the morning.

In the morning he took a little sports bag, hang it over his shoulder and left the house. He never left a letter, nor other thing, left the house quietly... Lisi wasn't sleeping, she jumped up, but before she dressed up, her brother was gone without the trace.

The boy with the rucksack was walking down the downtown. Accustomed to a constant care of his sister, is infinitely heart broken. Long highway is elongated on unbounded territory. He has passed his home city long time ago. He's going forward through inertial and unconscious. He took some rest. It got darker, lampions were shining slightly.

It's been just a five months he has practice football. Five months that he had dream and cherish has finished. He has left not only his home, his only family member, sister who had cared of him as a mother, but also football field... His favorite sport and has followed a new way without a trace. Sad as before and hopeless, as his hard and joyless childhood sorrow that has loaded his life at his early age.

Suddenly he has recalled camera. He has watched his photos. Here's Mtatsminda, here's Park de Vake, here's Qartlis Deda. Photo of Lizi has appeared too. The only photo... On the bed half turned aback and sleepy. He couldn't stand a sorrow and had thrown away the camera in the bushes. He lay down in the grass nor fear of darkness not of the possible attack of wild dogs or snakes... Nothing has scared him because of sadness all the other feelings were dead in him. Only sensation of missing and nostalgia... Nothing else...

Quite soon he jumped up. He started to look for the camera. He started to walk among the grass fumbling his hands in it. Suddenly he held something cold. He lifted it up. The shining green snake was hanging on his arm... He shouted once from the fear. He waved his arm strongly and threw it far, far away.

Unfortunately snake didn't bit him, as if he understood that the human being didn't mean to hurt him. But Lasha ran away, ran as hard as if the whole world was to catch him. He ran as fast as he could, as much as he could and finally stopped, he recalled the camera. I have to go back... I have to find it. I have to find it what ever it takes... Even if nothing else I've got there only one photo of my only one sister in the camera.

And the boy turned back. Where could he throw it? Will he be able to find it at all?.. He walked for half an hour, finally he got to that place, he recognized it, there were standing huge lampion on the left side to illuminate the street. He entered bravely into the grass. The fear has gone away, not by hand but by feet he started to fumble. In a few meters he choked with something rounded... "This is it... Yes, it's a camera..." The joy made him to forget tiredness and the sorrow. He opened his rucksack and kept it very carefully. He walked on further. For some time he walked joyfully. Then he recalled Lizi again. Lizi... Business and pragmatic sister... She's looking for him probably. She's looking for and who knows how grieve and sad she is. Thinking of this he sighed heavily and to avoid importunate thoughts started to run...

The boy with a bag on his shoulder was crossing the downtown street. Accustomed to his sister's perpetual care his heart was broken. There was not even a moment of some kind of remark from his sister, she had never mentioned a single reproach. That's why it hurt him so much. Lizi realized her mistake it was too much from her. She wanted to make him return the money, but Lasha was against it. Fourteen years old boy preferred to leave the house forever than to return the money. He didn't know where he was going, he just walked away down the road and the road is long from the outcome of the earth to it's end and you never know where the end can bring you.

Chapter 8

Two years passed since that day. Sister heard nothing about Lasha. First she was looking for in homeland, in every city and region. When she assured that the boy was not on Georgian territory, then she started to look for him in foreign countries... She sent letters to corresponding instances. Some of them never answered to her and some for just a formula wrote her that she had to produce union wide searching. To cut a long story short, somehow, she couldn't figure a way out, she realized that silly expectation couldn't help it and she had to do something. She didn't know what, but she wasn't made for inaction so she started to act. Brother's leaving home was a huge tragedy for her. First she bought Jeep of Nissan. Then she started to travel in different towns and regions. Relatives were seeing her dressed like a boy with the wig on her head more and more times.

"If only I could see him in my dreams, Oh, how I miss him..." Their cousine was fine. It was great of course, but she lost her brother? And she doesn't know if she'll ever find him? She spends nights crying, in the morning, she goes to job sleepy. In the evening she used to go to "Sioni" cathedral, and prays for Lasha. Only if she could know he is alive or not. "How could he do such a thing to me" thinks Lizi and enters brother's room, takes his clothes and books, cares them and talks to them.

She found a notebook in the box, it was Lasha's diaries. She glimpsed last notes. He wrote it a week before leaving the house. Lizi sat down and started to reed.

"Today Natia told me that she'll marry me when she is back from Europe. I never asked her to marry me. But I truly love her. It's interesting to see Lizi's face when she'll see Natia's long horsehair braids. She's funny my Natia, but anyway I love her." It was the end of the note. "Who is Natia? May be there is the way to find out, may be she knows something?" Lizi cherished a hope in a heart. Than she started to look for a camera, she couldn't find it. – He brought his camera with him – she thought and felt some kind of relief.

At night she dreamed her father. With a huge Newspaper in his hands he was sitting in an armchair and was looking at her above his glasses.

Don't cry my child! It's nothing... Do you see this? – He put his finger on the newspaper. He was indicated a drawing that was similar to map.

Take my binocular, don't forget it. – Said he and disappeared.

Lizi jumped up as a lunatic, Father, dream, brother... Fighting with a brother, shouting voices, Lasha's go away and disappearance. All of it was mixed with one another. She was clearly seeing the map drawing that her father showed to her. She took a good look on it. Then she took an atlas from the drawer, opened it and stood still, than she turned on the computer. She was almost sure that her brother was in Spain, she dropped tears of joy. The most wanted country for now showed on a white screen lighted her mind and her life.

My brother is alive. He is here. Yes he is here... Father told me. It's true, - She took on the T-shirt up side down and stayed in the computer. It seemed like the one she saw in her dream. No, it didn't seem like, but it was exactly it. With some oval shaped borders. She wrote down all information about this city even a climate and geographic location, because it was the most pleasant job for her to do right now. The place that she dreamed about such a long time, was right here, the place where her beloved brother was...

Chapter 9

It's all surrounded by green fields. There are wide fields at both sides of the road. Although there are bushes and trees here and there. Time after time some single cars overshot the road. It seems like this is the connecting road of those European and Asian countries between which is impossible to travel by sea. There's traffic all day, some cars drive for night also, although one can only notice the car is near by his headlights in the dark. You are passing through the endless distance blindly. Some times when you're lucky moonlight is shining your way, this is the most appropriate moment to walk fast and restless.

When he turned right he hid behind the bush at once. It is really very comfortable to hide here. The coming car is seen from the far away. Until it comes closer you can run and hide in the forest. He got the hand of doing it. Several days he is hiding from the people this way... some times when there are lots of cars he sleeps somewhere under the open sky. Eating, well what can we say about eating? he has not eaten for few days. He's got nothing in the bag but clothes. He's got camera on his shoulder. He doesn't take the pictures, his head was full with other problems, but he had it on his shoulder anyway.

Green field reminded him of his aunt and cousins. Ani, that is very ill. For saving her he wasn't ashamed before nothing, for her he left a house, beloved sister... But he doesn't regret anything, let Ani be well. He loves Lizi like a mother. And Ani and Tika like sisters... "Anyway what would we do if Nika didn't give us the money? Wouldn't we kill the girl, we had to do something?... I wonder how is she now?.. Had they have an operation or not?..."

He sat on his knapsack and watched the road. He remembered their village visiting again to his aunt. One summer while they were in village neighbour kids came for them. We are going to find some mushrooms and they asked if they would come as well. Lasha looked at Lizi as always. Lizi gave a sign to him by eyes to go if he wanted to,. She and Tika stayed at home, and Lasha and Ani went with the other kids with joy. "Village kids are very strange, garrulous and gossipers." Lasha was laughing at their speech, wrangling and rural dialect. It seemed like they were wise people and not kids competing with one another in expressions.

Lasha learnt a lot then, recognizing the mushrooms, coniferous trees and birds. Ani taught him then how to recognize the grass one can use for food. She took Lasha to the flourished field and if in the deepest childhood her little heart could foresee something she told him:

- When hopeless traveler gets lost and can't find his way home, when he is hungry and thirsty, he eats this grass. It feels person with energy. Kills his thirst and the hunger disappears. – Lasha was surprised by her wise thoughts, looked at her attentively and asked:

- How do you know that? –

- Uncle Sandro told me. Once he had lost in the forest too, and if not this grass he would die with hunger and thirst. –

Lasha laughed from the bottom of his heart. Suddenly he asked: How does it call Ani?

Ani was taken aback but she was representing herself as someone who knows everything so she didn't want to say I don't know, she hanged her head down, touched her front then looked at Lasha's face and said:

- This grass?... wait, I'll tell you... – and suddenly she made up: - "Pana" it's name is "Pana"

Lasha understood that Ani had told a lie, but didn't want to afflict her and to exclaim the surprise by her knowledge lifted his eyebrows. Ani was then very ridiculous. Lasha smiled having recalled her face expression. He became on good mood. As Ani was older then he was, as from an adult girl even lies were possible to trust and because of it she looked at the boy with top.

Now Lasha also recalled how Ani got tired by walking on foot. Other children headlong rose on a slope and Ani rose with respites, laboured for breath and often stopped. Who knew at that time the child had a heart disease. Lasha again grew dark. His heart began to creak on again. Also hunger and thirst have prevailed. To a fur-tree standing costs, still hardly scarcely was on his feet and will faint, can find to me this invented by Ani "Pana" and started to go on among a grass. At the same time his heart was captured by melancholy, joyful melancholy. Very little for him had remained to tears.

He sat down on a stone near by. He recalled mother vaguely and the father too, those minutes when in day of funeral the friend of her mother in haste of a visor took him away fast as she protected the boy from something. As he learnt after, parents have been buried side by side on a Vake cemetery. He recalled that as for the second day instead of mother he was woken by the aunt: "get up we will have breakfast". Lasha began to cry bitter tears when couldn't see mother, he didn't let anybody to approach, - 'leave me' he shouted. In the end he lifted his head, took in everybody at a glance and from the top of all his forces he ran to Lizi. Held her strongly, Lizi started to caress him. It was a sensation as if he was caressed long by mother. He calmed down but then the others began to cry: the Aunt, Ani, Tika, and a wide range of relatives.

After that he was adjoined to Lizi... Thoughts have drawn him upon the melancholy. Suddenly he shook a head and rose. He looked at the sky, not only his body was eremite on this boundless earth, but he also is a lonely soul.

He again shouldered the backpack and continued a way. Tired of a long journey. Not as worried for hunger as for thirst And insult caused by fight with his sister and repentance. Insult, missing and repentance. He felt that no longer could overcome himself. For all over the time he had his house in front of his eyes, routine, care of sister and even if orphanage but warm home atmosphere.

May be he should turn back... The same road, which he came by... But in the same second as if he beat off from thoughts, shook a head and quickly went forward.

The fourteen-year old boy himself felt that in him still there were elements of the childhood and that now occurred in his heart was similar to fight of two people, one of them thirsts for the sea and another for land, but both cases had the justification. In the end the victory was gained by that adult boy who was restless by insult and vanity and persistently continued his way.

Seemed like will grow misty. The rain should go. Lasha now goes not by road but in forest and a grass. He looked at a grass and it seemed to him that he saw onions-pares, in other grass he thought he saw greens which fill a string bean and which he often saw on a table... But he searched for exactly the invented by Ani "Pana." These memories heated his heart, connected him to his families, "Pana" "Pana" was his obsession, he had not to search for long, found it near a tree. He broke it and peered, at first slowly crumpled it in hands, then tasted, when he understood that it was not too bad, broke all in fists, he chewed and swallowed juice. It was pleasant to him and even was sated to a measure. Not far he noticed a raspberry. It was so pleasant for him that his face shined. He approached to it closer and broke, ate tirelessly, then took in armfuls and continued his way.

Chapter 10

In the evening in the open-air he lay down in one secluded place, put a backpack under a head and fell asleep at once. In the morning when the sun shined to him in eyes, he jumped up, he felt badly, he stroked his face. Suddenly he captured a terrible itch, he started to scratch all body with both hands. At night he was bitten by mosquitoes so much that all his body was covered by red stains. What horror, how come that I hadn't felt nothing? Really did I sleep so strong? He scratched so much, he almost took away the skin.

Again a wide valley... Some crops like water-melons on wide territory, approached and saw that the earth is covered by ripe water-melons. Should eat but how? He doesn't have a knife or other sharp subject. But it's no problem... He quickly made up his mind... In the same place he broke a branch and the sharp end made an incision on a surface, the ripe water-melon revealed a red strip, started to eat, ate until he has not felt weight in a stomach.

He followed his way. How would he be able to find out how much remains to the nearest settlement? How many days should it take to come to some city. If only I could pass through border. Nobody can cross it without the permission and the documents. He was carried away by these thoughts when he saw the wide river which dissected road on two parts "At the river there must be the bridge and that will be probably at border." No... How would he get to the border... Who will let him cross the border... Better to him to cross the river and in such way to continue his way. And if not then he must return the same road back. "No way, I will not turn back." He sharply solved it in his heart. "How should I act farther?". He was terrified; he is not a bird to fly over?

He can swim but he doesn't dear to go into the river? Suddenly he made up his mind. He grubbed his bag and ran into forest, he lowered branches of trees, hardly broke off a little from them, then he broke them, put on the earth and collected something like a raft, then he broke off two big branched out branches for oars. He shifted a backpack through a shoulder and rose on a raft. Weight of a body made him move in one part of the raft, so the boy nearly fell in the river, but to keep balance he bent in an opposite side and rowed, so that the raft floated. He's now absolutely close to the coast, now even if he would turn over he can reach for roots of trees and reaches to the land. The original raft of wooden branches made by Lasha stuck to the coast, he jumped and rose on the earth, suddenly a raft turned over and floated on a surface, then the current incurred it downwards. The rescued boy spent a raft with a grateful look and as though the stone from shoulders sighed with simplification.

In the afternoon the huge bus appeared on the road. He felt the bus occurrence when it was already very close. Confused started to do awkward movements, ran in the left then in the right. Then crossed the road directly and went down on a slope. He was afraid of police, as he had crossed the border without the permission. Fourteen years old minor child doesn't have control over any documents so one cannot be surprised if he escapes from people. He does not know what he will do when comes to a city. The only thing he knows is that in the first city he should find a shelter for the night.

He heard the sound of the approached autobus and soon the driver braked the car. The boy with fear grew to a bush and stood still. He heard shout of women from the bus.

- Help. Police... - women shouted. People spread out from the bus and started to search the boy.

- This little bastard could put a mine, or some explosive material otherwise why does he have to escapes why does he hide? - Passengers could not calm down.

Some of them had such a cold look, especially men and children sitting in the bus as some kind of insensible bodies have been put on chairs. Adults apparently were apathetic and children looked at such things coolly. They only wish to see and hear funny, entertaining stories... Why do they have to care about the nobility destiny of the boy met on road, secret of his runaway or why he hides? They sit on soft chairs of the bus and do not take away a cold look from passengers.

One busty woman in small shorts of average years with a fast pace approached to a slope and in broken Italian started to shout (on appearance she decided that the boy was Italian). When she was convinced that the boy continued standing and hiding silently behind a bush she decided that he's not the Italian and started to shout in English.

Lasha was in a trap. There was no way out, he had to leave a hiding place... He rose and staggered out to people, he timidly looked at the woman's eyes and answered with perfect English:

- Do not shout at me madam! I am innocent - tears have begun to flow at the boy's face, the young boy which left the bus, approached to him, took him by a hand and ordered to go with them, but in his heart thought: "What if he's not guilty but simply lost the way that's all..." He has led him to the bus, Lasha has resign to his fate, what else could he do. "what should happen it would happen" and rose to the bus. As without booking and guilty they made him stand, the majority of passengers were observing him with suspicion examined him serially, and the busty fat woman did not took her angry eyes from him and was mattering for herself.

As he understood while standing there, it was the day off and some corporate group of employees went on a beach to have a rest... And here this boy, (which can even be searched by the police) had spoilt their celebratory spirit. The day off, walk on a small coastal city, it was a dream for all the whole week, and the busty woman prepared specially for this day so she could not calm down for a long time, she buzzed all ears to the next sitting man.

Soon the young man who brought him to the bus let him have his sit, stood nearby and carried on a conversation with him. His attention, warm attitude to him was pleasant for Lasha, at least one person took him into consideration, it's not so bad. It was such a relief. When the bus stopped at a small market, the young man bought him an ice-cream and put to his hands a small bottle of Coca-Cola... It made Lasha felt awkward, but he wanted ice-cream so much that he took it and looked at him with such grateful eyes that meant that he felt protected in hands of such defender.

- You travel to take photos? – He asked not for a curiosity but for the sake of rapprochement of the new acquaintance, at the same time looked at the camera on a lap of the boy.

- I like to take photos - Smiled Lasha. The boy smiled at him in the answer. After that they became friends. The boy was called Bobbi. "I am twenty two" - he thought. "The same age that my sister" - Lasha thought and a very little kept him to not to embrace him, not to hold him in his arms.

Nothing disturbs him any more. Even if the police will catch him, he's overflowed with hope from care of this boy. He recalled Lizi, recalled and understood how much he missed her and after a while hiding his face in hands he bitterly began to cry.

There were a lot of people on the shore. Bobbi picked up the moment, took Lasha by a hand and whispered to him that they had to go. While the busty woman who had already forgotten the shameless boy and history of unpleasant travel and very happy rejoiced now by looking at the sea from the shore. Bobbi and Lasha had cozy sits on taxi armchairs rushed on the way to Madrid.

Chapter 11

The new acquaintance appeared was the Englishman. He was sent to work in Spain. He was so kind, so paternal in relation to Lasha that took the boy in his rented apartment. The small two-room apartment was decorated by small furniture. He treated the boy with a hamburger and hotdog, found out some things about him. Lasha answered avariciously his questions. Bobbi learnt that he was the orphan, that his parents were lost in plain accident. That in his native city foreigners came seldom and its country almost connected by nothing with Europe. When Bobbi asked him about relatives, Lasha answered that he did not have almost any relatives except cousins of the father that he saw last time on funeral of the parents, then he became silent again and never spoke to him about that. He kept silence about sister and cousin sisters.

Bobbi made him a bad into a living room, he fell asleep as soon as he closed eyes. For the second day Bobbi looked long on him sleeping some time with pity and on other hand with suspicion. He even tried to wake him up by shaking or even crying on him but could not wake him. He slept as cut down from a medicine. Well he left to him the letter on a kitchen table that he could take meal from a refrigerator, read the book, watch the TV, and at five o'clock he would come back home.

When Bobbi came back home he found the boy still sleeping. Surprised took a long look at him. Came closer to listen. The boy breathed easy and rhythmically. "So much to sleep" he thought, but recalled that the boy went on foot for very long time, so the recreation is necessary not only for economy and the countries, but also "people require to restore forces and rest" he thought and put a laptop box on a table, turned on the gas and went in a bathroom. Suddenly phone rang and it was Jenita.

- You have returned my love – He said and then added

- I have a surprise for you, I will acquaint you with one foreign boy, - come to my place. -

- What foreigner boy? - Jenita has burst out laughing.

- This is what you'll find out when you come, can you arrive as soon as possible?

- I will arrive... - Jenita continued to laugh loudly. Bobbi hanged up.

"I hope he'll wake up in one hour, the sleepyhead". Has thought and counted the time for himself "He sleeps sixteen hours" whistled and went to the bathroom.

Everything was as usual in the refrigerator. He was hungry and put everything he found in it on the table. He put sausage on it, then cheese, a tomato, mayonnaise, cetchup on the big piece of bread and then started to eat with such impulse as someone pursued him. He wished to eat before Jenita came because one of the most beautiful girls of Madrid, his bride and the friend, because of weight problems was on the strict diet again...

Chapter 12

The first what Lasha saw when he opened his eyes, it was the silhouette of the woman by the window. Suddenly he couldn't figure out where he was, he recalled Lizi and nearly called her, but at once he understood that it was not Lizi. Meanwhile he came to the senses. When he recalled everything, he felt so badly, suddenly the missing of the house embraced his feelings, that he turned to a back and began to cry in a pillow. His still not formed age, gave him a chance to express grief childishly. He was just fourteen years old. When he cried a river he got up. Jenita and Bobbi were looking at him with a sorrow. Jenita turned to Bobbi. She was looking at him for a long time with questions in her eyes, from surprise both stood silently. Eventually Bobbi said:

- Leave us for a while Jeni - And he turned to Lasha

- Why do you cry? - he asked sympathetically. It was quite enough for the grieving child to begin crying and hang in a pillow more deeply. Bobbi did not ask anything more. He just told him in low tones:

- All right, it's ok... see, everything's fine, it is my girlfriend, she has come to meet you. Won't you get up? -

Lasha slowly ceased to cry, silently turned and led eyes round on a room full with the tears, then he looked at Bobbi, he nodded him, then jumped on feet and began to dress up.

- You can take a bath if you want to, as I see you have not bathed for a long time. Lasha nodded on everything. Jenita entered the room and smiled at him friendly. Lasha smiled at her in the answer. Then he entered the bathroom with the backpack in which he had pair of clothes and an album with photos made on excursion,

That day how much it was possible to get know to each other and to get closer they did and they became closer friends and became happier. In the evening they took the boy in cozy country restaurant. Lasha already felt perfectly. He knew English well and he felt a beat pleasantly. The laughter of Jenity reminded him of his sister, so he strangely stared on her so that Bobbi happened to blow him on a back, and told him:

- What, are you falling in love with my bride boy? - Lasha reddened and hung a head, and Jenita and Bobbi laughed with all their hearts.

Eventually the boy adapted to foreign environment, for the second day Bobbi put some books on shelves for him and told him:

- Reed these books. Mean while you'll stay here, then you'll find a way by yourself. Lasha took one book first than another. He had not read in English before, especially with such "a thick cover and big". "Lizi forced him to read too" - he thought and despite a reluctance to read this similarity pleased him. How all people look like each other. Jenita looks like Lizi when she laughs; Bobbi does with his care about him just like Lizi. Probably all adults are such kind and started to read to make Bobbi pleasantly.

The detective novel "Adventure of Avakum Zakhov" resulted to be very pleasant for reading. The expressed talent and character of the hero impressed him. Carried away by reading he did not notice as Bobbi had entered the room at all. Suddenly he jumped on feet.

Bobbi was pleased by his cultural behavior and was also pleased to see him with the book in hands. Happily, he nodded a head, took him in a glance from feet to head.

Lasha was almost her height. Bobi turned to the room and in few minutes, he came out with clothes in his hands.

- Lasha! Here are trousers and T-shirts, put on, I think they are of your size and you will use them. Lasha thanked him and nodded politely.

- Now let's get some rest, common we'll have dinner. - The kitchen table was full of fruits, and there were boiled sausages on glass plates that smelled very pleasantly.

Let's have a main meal first and then fruits. The apple is very useful - Bobbi cheerfully swung hands. Laha looked at a vase full of fruits, words of Bobbi and a vase fool of fruits reminded him of home. Lizi always brought peaches and apples. Peaches were much tasty but Lizi always asked to eat an apple too. Here is also the same story about good of apples... After all everything is similar to each other, it stands to reason and it's natural... "Levelling of events is impossible..." He recalled it from one book he had read before and suddenly felt freedom, the same as it is in Georgia, with his sister.

- Eat, what are you waiting for?– The voice of Bobbi awaked him from thoughts, he brought a plug with a sausage to a mouth, Bobbi already ate up his share and stood on the feet.

- I have to go now I'm late, read the book and don't open the door to anybody. - Lasha suddenly ceased to eat and confusedly rose. Bobbi smiled to him and said cheerfully:

- Continue don't get up, we're friends, aren't we? - And went out quickly.

It is the truth Bobbi is his friend now and also the patron, but it seems to Lasha that he's very much respective concerning to him. Well the fact that he treated kindly, is not an occasion to behave unworthy. He is not his relative; he's a stranger to him. He don't have to shelter and sponsor him. He has to obey to behave well, to read books and if it's required to risk his life for him. To the lines characterizing nature of the Georgian person the time, the distance and the foreign environment can't do any harm, conceived as the adult clever man, Lasha does not try to feel on equal high with Bobbi or imagine himself as his friend... Also thinks to thank him on a merit and after that to leave Bobbi's house peacefully as soon as possible.

Chapter 13

When he remained alone in the evening, when Janita and Bobbi had gone to the cinema to watch movie, he was captured by melancholy. He's not going to return, but even if he decides to return it will be impossible as he doesn't even know how he got here, he spent many nights and days in the open-air before he met Bobbi, he doesn't even know how many. Then he got really lucky. He has not got in hands of police but in hands of the kind person which sheltered him as relative. He sheltered and didn't feel ashamed to take care of him. Never has suspected that this small teenager could be some kind of criminal that the police searched, After all the busty woman in shorts did look at him with suspicion and disgust. Here where he got so easily by assistance of Bobbi, considers himself the lucky person. If not Bobbi that woman would hand him over to police and who knows what would happen to him. If he could avoid a colony they would send him in orphanage, and in the best case they would send him back homeland.

He recalled something what made him feel better, he went to the phone, picked up the receiver and meditate. He did not know how to call in Georgia, just knew that it needed to type a code of Georgia. There were plenty of things near the phone – numbers of transport service and different other firms. He rang few times here and there. Suffered much, in the end he called in the information service and asked a code of Georgia, he called home but in vain. He knew exactly, if Lizi lifted the receiver he would not answer and would hang it up. "Then why do I call?" the boy asked "just so" answered to himself.

After that always when he remained home alone he was calling to Georgia, some times it worked out some times not. Once some man took the receiver, but it meant that he got the wrong number...

But since he has started these strange calls something happened in his life, something rejoices and makes him feels perfectly, this sincere inclination connects him with his home, with a native city, with beloved sister. It's right it is not real communication but is supplied by hope, the hope which has been not realized and is simply pleasant.

Janita and Bobbi got used to the boy so much that when they where out they always asked each other where the boy can be now. One evening they came back home late, the door of the flat was left opened and Lasha was out. In horror they examined all district streets and court yard even on plaza but he couldn't be found nowhere. They thought that he had run away and it made them very sad. Many times Jenita was asking to Bobbi where he could be... Bobbi was silent, he sincerely regretted. Suddenly the door ball rang. Lasha was on the threshold with his camera in hands and was looking at them with guilty eyes.

- Come in, why do you stand there, where have you been? – He griped the scared boy's arm and brought him in the flat as he was stuck in the doorway as a statue.

- Where have you been? - They asked again simultaneously.

- I was taking pictures of the city with from the roof. - Bobbi sighed with relief. He asked if he could take a look on them. Lasha gave him a camera, he went to a room himself. Night streets illuminated by lampions and the house areas plunged into greens were a delightful show... Jenita could not constrain the admiration. Lasha brought an album out from a room that he had brought from Georgia. The Georgian churches and ancient quarters of Tbilisi, it was unusual to see. Suddenly they saw a photo of sleeping Lizi.

- Who's the girl? - Bobbi asked. Lasha was confused and blushed. Couldn't say anything. Bobbi could understand that Lasha had some secret in heart that he was not giving away with him. That there was some secret reason for him to leave homeland and go by feet to other land and postponed the conversation for some other time.

Chapter 14

Lasha was reading through nights, and slept till the late morning. For evenings he was going out with his camera on a backyard to walk. From there one could see apple trees, pears and different fruit along the whole way in the right side. Nearby there was a fancy house and on that house's terrace once, he noticed an old man. The man was smoking a cigarette and with other hand was attaching a branch to a picket. When he saw the boy he smiled at him as a relative and waved him to come closer to him. Lasha couldn't move away his eyes from the stranger who was already going down from a stairs limping. Lasha remembered that he lived in a city illegally that he should hide and avoid people as Bobbi had also told him and tried to get away, but could not avoid the confidant it was too late. The stranger shaked his big and fat hand with the boy and then said to him in Spanish. Lasha answered him in English and the man was a bit surprised by his answer.

- Are you an Englishman? – He asked with surprise. Lasha hung a head, but he didn't tell him anything. The man continued:

- Would you help me to collect apples, I have hurt my feet - Lasha has slowly lifted a head, looked at heaps of apples and stirred up his shoulders. The man got a role of money from the pocket and showed a pack of Euros.

- I'll pay you money, sixty Euros a day, it is not a small amount – This proposal made Lasha shine, but did not show pleasure, waited a little then nodded a head as a sign of agreement.

The man brought out the big iron ladder from a cellar and put to an apple tree. Lasha recalled village again and the aunt and cousin sisters. Lizi... Lizi whom he misses very much... There is no time for this now... The Man seemed like had read his thoughts, looked at him intently. Lasha got lost, but tried not to show. He rose on a ladder and in one second he appeared at the top of it.

The man was glad about his adroitness and flexibility, smiled at him and showed him a bucket. Lasha returned as quickly as he had gotten up, took a basket and returned upstairs. In just five minutes returned downwards with a fool bucket. In two hours he had collected eight buckets of apple. The surprised and satisfied owner of the garden looked at the boy with a smile, then he called somewhere. Big car arrived to the garden, loaders got out of there and placed flanks full of apples on the car body and carried it away somewhere.

It got almost dark. Charles came to Lasha sitting on the little bench and gave him his sixty Euros.

- Come to help me tomorrow, come earlier. Tomorrow I will give you more money, you're a good boy. Now go – he said and for goodbey, he again gave him his big thick hand. Lasha hardly smiled of weariness, took money and went home.

On the second day as soon as Bobbi left for work, he got up at once, put on his clothes and ran to the garden, so proceeded one week until Bobbi was back home. He worked until he drop down from weariness in the next garden, collecting apples and pears. But he couldn't read the book any more because at night when he came back home he fell strongly asleep.

The owner of the garden liked the little boy very much. Surprised by his daring he tried to learn more about him. Lasha wasn't so talkative, he told him that he is an orphan and then became silent, as at conversation with Bobbi... The Man told him about himself that he was lonely and had two houses in the city that he had to look after the both houses serially. It was not much joy to have two houses for the widow and lonely man, not there not here, he said that he could not find rest, but he could not sell one and so he suffered to rush about there and here, so he spent his life time to walk between two houses that's all. And then he smiled. Suddenly he was captured by fatherly feeling to him. As it seemed he had his own plans about Lasha. He's been watching all over him all day long as if he tried to study his character, did not get away from him not for one step.

When the job was done Charles gave him an envelope with money in such a stately manner as it was an award for world war hero.

- I am waiting for you tomorrow - He said, and stretched him his big thick hand again. Lasha smiled. Eight hundred Euros deserved by his own work was not so little money for the little boy and happy and joyful, he went home as fast as possible.

Chapter 15

In the morning Lasha put a clean sheet of paper on the table. After thinking for a while what to write... looked at watch, it was nine o'clock. There was no time to think, so he rose and quickly inscribed on a paper:

"Thank you Bobbi! Forgive me that I didn't not warn you. I am leaving now He didn't even take the money from the envelope, and left on the table with the letter and with his bag on the back left the house. It was hard for him to leave the house where he had spent six months with the kind person. He was very sorry that had not warned Bobbi the night before, that he was leaving without any warning so shameless.

There was a white jeep standing near the house of the garden owner. The driver stood nearby and drank a yellow liquid from a huge bottle, and Charles in sportswear and with sunglasses in hands stood near by the car. When he saw Lasha his face became cheerful, opened the door widely to him and suggested to take a sit. Soon the car passed by the house of Bobbi, Lasha sadly looked at the house, two metal-plastic windows coming out on street and silently sighed. Now the third and possibly the heaviest period of his life was beginning for him which prepared him for even bigger and variety difficulties.

Charles was in high mood, laughed and spoke with the driver on unknown for Lasha Spanish language. Sometimes probably for Lasha's sake he spoke on broken English. Lasha understood that he spoke with the driver about a hurt foot and about the big crop. The rich crop certainly was a source of pleasure for him, but cheerful conversation about a hurt foot (that was not so pleasant reality for a crippled man) was not so clear.

They drove about an hour so Charles hadn't stopped talking not for a minute, smoked a cigarette behind a cigarette, strewed ashes on an orange T-shirt, but it seemed that he didn't care about that so much. He was only sorry that all life he tried to give up smoking but he couldn't.

The driver sat silently, it was evident that he was the reticent person. He belonged to that category of people which do not love opposes, which expresses both the consent and refusal with silence.

When the jeep stopped at a big, blue house, Lasha had time to think that the man belonged to a rich layer, that he could take more skilled and adult person as an assistant instead of this little boy. But as it seemed he had a different point of view on life, considerably various and for him it was principally to take not skilled boy like Lasha demanding to formalize than the generated typical man of all trades.

There was a big dog tight in the yard, which began to bark as soon as the car stopped at the house door. Charles opened a car door, left lamely, approached to the dog and stroked him, stroked on furry wool. Then he led Lasha to the door.

- Who might live with him - Lasha thought, and had just thought it when from kitchen entered a thin woman of average years who seemed to be a servant. Charles approached to her closer and told her something in Spanish, probably about the boy because the woman secretly looked at Lasha.

- I'll bring a breakfast right away – The servant said and went to the kitchen. As he learnt later, the woman's name was Flora. She had a very kind expression. Beautiful eyes and eyebrows have been raised upwards with proud, but her nature seemed to be very soft and obedient. The servant understood that the boy had more reputation in Charles's consideration than an ordinary apprentice to which one shouldn't trust too much. She looked at the boy with great attention, smiled at him and then took his bag. She told him "this way please" and led him to a bathroom. Soon she appeared from kitchen doors bringing the big tray with a breakfast for two, coffee with milk, chocolate and cakes that meant that Charles and the unfamiliar boy should have breakfast on one in the living room.

Chapter 16

Lasha woke up early in the morning. He heard a noise, sat on the bad and listened. It was the sound of the rain, not a sound but noise. A downpour poured on a roof. He got up and looked out of a window. All around was immersed that it seemed as the river left a channel. He dressed up quickly and went downstairs. The breakfast was already served by the servant and she sat on a chair with a tired expression. When she saw the boy she cheered up and greeted him with a smile. Lasha began to sparkle at the sight of her smile and he dared to ask about Charles.

- Charles have gone to the city, he said that he would return tomorrow – The woman answered in correct English to the English speaker boy. Lasha thought at once that his new owner was the business and pragmatic person. Probably he went on very important issue – He thought and sat down on a small chair standing nearby.

- Go to the bathroom and have a breakfast then. What is your name? - Flora asked the boy.

- Lasha. –

- I hear this name for the first time. -

- It is a Georgian name. - "Georgian" repeated Lasha under letters.

-Are you Georgian? Yes, I have heard. It's Russia right? –

- No, madam, it's Georgia - Lasha interrupted and wrinkled a forehead. Georgia became the independent state just two or three years ago. For this purpose all Georgian people - adults and children self-denyingly struggled in its country. Of course the Georgian teenager had claims out of all it.

- I was named after our king called Lasha-George - Lasha continued with pride overflowing in his voice. Like saying I am Georgian and my name is royal name. He recalled history lessons when the teacher explained to them about a kingdom of Lasha-George of the son of Queen Tamar.

He even remembered years. He reigned in 1213-1223 and the not talkative boy as if he just learnt to speak, continued the tale.

- It was the son of Queen Tamar, have you heard about Tamar? - Flora hadn't heard about her and shook a head negatively.

- You know about Michael Saakashvili? Heard about Michael? - Lasha was grown bolder by the mentioning of the president.

Flora began to shine.

- I know, I know, tall one, beautiful one... -

- Yes, it's him... tall and beautiful. It's my president. -

Flora suddenly stared.

- You look like him - the Saakashvili, eyes, a nose, yes you do... -

The woman could not hide the admiration. She looked at him so respectfully as it was a real president of Georgia in front of her. After this she hadn't spoken much, she silently invited the boy to the table and if she was late somewhere, went to the room upstairs.

Lasha had breakfast. He had somehow unusual sensation. He wanted to go out to the yard and to take a walk. First he examined near by places and the next houses.

Then he approached to a dog. He stood not far from it and started at it. Soon surprised departed back. The dog had such expressive eyes that it seemed to him that some person was looking at him. The dog pulled to him. Flora consulted him not to get too close, because the dog has changeable character some times it was harmless and safe and then terrible and mad. Lasha understood that such a clever dog could not be all over the world because it was very similar to someone very close to the boy as like as two peas.

That night when Lasha fell asleep at the open window the dog called "Max" climbed to it from the window and slept at his feet all night long on the floor, and in the morning before Lasha had woken up, it furtively slept away out of the room as a professional thief.

Every night, when the dog was free out of collar and was let go to protect the house and when it felt freedom it was disappearing somewhere and was coming back only at a sunrise. These strangenesses have started to occur since Charles had returned from extreme Madrid house together with Lasha. It was strange but this strangeness was supplemented by more shocking which nobody else could notice except Lasha. The dog reacted to everything as clairvoyant, as a living soul to which there were many strange things... And what is the main and most essential is that the dog "dangled after" Charles's new tenant foreign "traveler boy" all the time, from the sunrise to the sunset.

As Bobbi came back home he found the letter on the table. He was confused with surprise, "What can it be?" Also took a small piece of a paper in hands. He could not believe to his eyes. He looked around. He was excited. Where could the boy go? Why would he go? He was so disturbed by this that could not notice an envelope on a table at all. He started to walk around. Then he went to the phone and called to Jenite. Nobody answered. Suddenly he noticed an envelope on the table. He approached and what?...There is money in the envelope... Eight hundred Euros... "What is it...When did the boy have money... From where? He had not a stiver while he was with him. Where could he take it? Who could give to him such sum?

It was exactly the sum that Bobbi had to pay for rent for two months, tomorrow exactly tomorrow he has to pay for the flat rent. There was a small card next to the money. Now he opened this card. All was surrounded with such a mystery the letter on the table, the letter in the envelope. Someone called Charles Mendoza was signing the card. As soon as he read he hardened. The excitement and surprise was expressed on his face.

All is clear - he said and looked towards the road which was leading to gardens.

The sun slowly fell over the roof of Charles's houses.

Chapter 17

However, Lizi was repented very much with thoughts about his brother and often cried in lonely places and regretted that had behaved with him so severely, but she was so encouraged by thought that she would find and see him that she was the same habitual optimist. Nika called her for so many times and asked how Ani was doing. Ani already felt healthy, operation had passed successfully. Lizi was very surprised how Nika knew about Ani but Nika had left this question without the answer and asked:

- Can I do anything for you? - Lizi thanked him for attention, told him about family troubles and promised that she would see him before she departures out of border.

Nika was revolted and disturbed by disappearance of Lasha. He understood that the money he had given to him was the reason of the misunderstanding between sister and brother. But he was satisfied by the result. Ani was well. The small lovely creation, which Nika had seen before for few times at Lizi's place, was well. And Lasha is the boy and the grown up one. Sooner or later he will understand that he was a victim of childish silly quarrels and will come back home himself. Things like that often happened also to Nika he quarreled with his family for many times and later understood that he was the one who was guilty in everything... The same will be in Lasha's case. But Lizi... Poor Lizi... Even if she is the strong girl, fighting and strong-willed, but she's lonely anyway. She is alone and I should see her.

Nika suddenly revolved in opposite side. He went to the house of Lizi. He was in no mood, he accused himself that had given money to the teenager. How came that he had not thought about it... He had not guessed, to bring it by himself, to give money to Lizi by himself then this trouble would pass by the brother and sister. But there is no time for this kind of thoughts, I should see her right now... The childhood friend probably might need so much, the most important from the friend.

He could not even understand how he got at Lizi's door. He had walked quickly and restless. He could hardly breathe. When he rang on the doorbell, he looked around. he had not been here for some years. Nothing had changed here. In the corner of the left wall a ladder was leading in an attic, here it stood as always. Children many times rose on this ladder in an attic and thought out one thousand different games. "Oh" - gave up as a bad job and pressed the bell again. Expectation was long. Nobody opened the door. Where can she be... Where has she gone?. Suddenly he felt an awful regret. The conscience voice reminded him of obligations. "How could I leave Lizi. Little Lasha. I swear that I'll do anything, I'll even go on a crime just to see them happy if only the brother and sister could find each other again".

Suddenly he began to knock by hands as if so he could be heard better as it happened in the childhood when he couldn't rich out for a doorbell and endlessly knocked by fingers, in such way she made Lizi understand that it was him. Lizi was then immediately opening a door and spread a brightness of her eyes in his face:

- Are you out of your mind Nik! What are you knocking so much for?... - And laughing they came into the house. How he had not forgotten about it? Recalling all this he smiled. Recalling the childhood or because of this knocking gave to him a sensation of pleasure, he continued to knock. The next door was suddenly opened and the neighbor looked out of it.

- Lizi is not at home, who are you? - She asked and attentively looked at him in the eyes.

- I'm Nika Madam, Lizi's schoolmate. -

- Oh, Yes son, I hadn't seen her today - Nika thanked her and turned away and left at once. He called on the mobile as he was crossing the road. Then took a taxi and went in the direction of the Rustaveli Avenue.

There were too many people at the building of Central Post Office. Lizi was among them in the queue. It was a hot summer day. Air was stuffy and stood still. Who knows when her turn would come , but she doesn't give up... What a problem to stand a few hours... She could stand even more if only she could get from an embassy the permission to leave. If only she could leave the country.

- Though Lizi here handed over nerves here and tears appeared on her eyes... Why wouldn't they let her go?... Why can't she go to Spain?...What's wrong with it? Even if they would knew the trip reason. She is going to find her brother, not to kill somebody... Lizy hardly coped with thoughts... Who's business is it where she would go. Really aren't they enough in proofs of her honesty the inquiry from her Karate trainer and from her job? If after all she's going to be refused, She'll go to other place, will go anyway somewhere in other country and from there she will try to pass to Spain. Anyway, the decision is clear and firm, there is nothing that could make her to reject. She will go around the whole world step by step in search of the unique brother. On the native land there is already nothing that could hold her here.

But consulates certainly did not submit desires of Lizi and persuasive desires of people wishing to leave the country... They solved this kind of questions by their ways. Flow abroad of people in such massive image from the native land was quite inexcusable. But despite their Low, for intolerable conditions after the war, all who could or to whom the fate had smiled in the different ways went abroad. In the country such pauperism reigned that it could seem strange from outside, but the majority of the population was afflicted with desire to leave the country.

And here the turn of Lizi has come. The young blonde, asked a surname and smiled at her as to someone very close. She started to rummage among envelopes. Took one and so grandiosely handed over as though she knew that from the embassy of Turkey the affirmative reply had come. When Lizi saw a kind of arrangement of the employee of Post Office, she felt obliged and sincerely smiled at her not less in the answer and quickly left from there. She opened a card on her way. As soon as she opened a card, she nearly went out of her mind. My God!... This is an exit visa, it's here, It is right here!. She looked around searching someone with whom to share her happiness? She has looked at the visa again. She nearly cried out, but restrained and with fast, uncertain step went to an exit. Suddenly she sees Nika, Nika who went to her. Lizi went forward to him, embraced the child-hood friend and while they left a building she silently whispered to him:

- I have got the Viza Nika, the Viza... - Nika froze on a place, for a moment he could not say a word, then he regained consciousness and gave her a warmest kiss ever. Lizi did search with whom to share her happiness. What a lucky one she is?... With all passion took the boy for a hand and happily smiling they went towards the Rustaveli Avenue.

Chapter 18

Lizi paid to the teacher of the Spanish language last salary and said goodbye to her. When she approached to the house, she was called by the buyer of the car, he asked her address. Lizi checked pockets and luckily keys were with her, she went into the garage and led out the car in the street. Near the car she sat down at the wall and waited for the client. In ten minutes the client came. At first he well examined the car then passed by the car around, villages in it and got on the car, then quickly said:

- Tomorrow I will take it away in the morning – and left the place without saying the goodbye at all.

- I have sold the car I can already go... –She said to herself and went upstairs. For the second day according to the condition, the new owner of the car arrived to Lizi with the little boy, he quickly counted her money and easily left the garage on new black "jeep". Lizi put money in the pocket and crossed herself. Then she looked around the street and straightly (as though the last time) and proudly walked on the court yard.

Her birthday was coming. Lizi recalled this day having glanced in the passport. She's becoming twenty six years old... Twenty six years are not little for her. "I grow old" she thought... I am leaving on my birthday. - She murmured and opened clothes wardrobe. As my reader and I know, her only clothes were jeans and jackets, only sportswear; she took it all separately and put in a bag. She was just going to fall asleep, when she heard loud voices and swearing from the street.

She approached to the window and saw that in the yard of a restaurant near the house the people had gathered. There was such a noise and a din that happens in expectation of the big and awful fight. After a while some young men were allocated from the group and came to the direction of Lizi's house.. They have started to argue and fight directly in front of the building. It was visible that the drunk man had already had unpleasant conversation among themselves at the restaurant and now have gone out of doors to fight. Loud threatening voices were audible... The frightened tenants could not dare to approach to windows and secretly looked at a show through curtains and Lizi looked at this unpleasant scene having put out a head in the window. Suddenly one of the swearing noticed in the dark window Lizi and enraged cried in her way:

What the hell are you looking at, boy... Fuck you... –

It was enough for Lizi, she took her wig on at once and ran out on the street without looking back. The boys already were mixed in each other, it was impossible to understand who was beating whom or who was right and who was wrong. (Lizi always was interested in this question). The others were beating two fallen boys without mercy. Lizi jumped in directly from an entrance. It took her two jumps, joined the crowd of fighting boys, waved hands and feet in the air at the same time, and in just a minute the silence in the street was established... Pleasant silence.

Windows of the nine-floor building were already open widely and neighbors with pride and with a smile looked at Lizi.

- God bless you girl, you'll be blessed... - Their exclamations were heard.

Lizi deeply sighed, corrected the wig on the head and looked up. Having seen smiling neighbors she smiled too. Then she looked at guys falling on the earth from the top and told them:

This is for mentioning my lost mother boys, and (indicated up) for rest infringement these people have! I hope you'll remember it well. - told and turned away, she quickly ran upstairs. She politely passed by the people who had gathered at her door, wished them "good night" and closed the door behind her.

I hope it was my last fight here... She thought and looked on the watch it was one a. m.

- I will leave this place too... - She told to herself and looked in the room of Lasha, she looked on his bad...

- Lasha will sleep here again. You will see if not... – She threatened someone or something and started to search in computer. She started to collect the information about Spain once again and Spaniards. There was a sweet and pleasant picture before her eyes. Precisely such which is called imaginary. Madrid! And yet unknown houses and streets of Madrid.

In the majority deserted places. The old temple ruins, then the picture of how she's going to meet her brother. From the car of a white jeep as last time, when she struck her brother, when from his full of fury eyes some another man was looking at Lizi, she saw exactly the same sight, clearly and in real... But Lasha was the adult, very adult, with small beard and was very handsome.

Chapter 19

There were police cars at the cash desks. There was a noise and din all over the place. As it was found out later, two young women tried to pass the Turkey border with somebody else's passports. The cashier suspected something in authenticity of the passports and called the police. The women in vain tried to prove their innocence. They looked quite sincere but to prove the sincerity low-enforcers put them in the car and took them away somewhere. Lizi was shocked by this unpleasant show... Her documents are perfectly in order, she doesn't have a single counterfeit inquiry in her hands, the multiple winner on karate goes to other country. What can be there strange or suspicious? There is nothing. Suddenly she understood that it's her turn. The cashier looked at her with surprise.

Lizi suddenly regained consciousness and safely stretched the passport, and then money. In some minutes she went out of doors with tickets to Spain in her hands.

In two days Lizi departs. She goes there where nobody and nothing is waiting for her.

Nothing – reliable and nobody –to count on. But Lizi will leave anyway, will go there where she piously trusts that she will find her brother. She will find her beloved orphan brother, whom she had tremblingly grown up by herself. Probably he has already grown up and is the adult boy... If he looks like their father - tall and handsome Valiko with big beautiful eyes and high forehead, because none of them looks like their mother...her parents appeared in front of Lizi's sight. She turned sad and to avoid these thoughts she started to put her clothes in the box.

She has already put all important things in a small bag, and has added the wig and the field-glass of her father on the top of the big bag. He put the bag in the hall and went to her aunt to say good bay. The aunt cried for a while, and begged her to look after herself with more prudence. Ani and Tika cried too. Lizi gave them a long hug eventually she shed few tears too and hastened, turned quickly and left. She went on the road fast. Absolutely alone and lonely... She once again merged with cruel and not clear reality that come to her life long ago.

It was hot. It was so stuffy that she took off a thin jeans jacket and went along to the direction of the Bank's. Soon she went out, bought dry food in shop round the corner and returned back home...

In the morning when she closed the door with a bag in her hands stood for a long time silently very sad. Then she touched the door with her fingertips, spent a hand on the handle and suddenly... To the only witness of her departure, to only sharer of her joy and sorrow, she whispered something to it. Whispered and hotly kissed... kissed as the person, as someone very close... Then she quickly came downstairs without looking back so that nobody could see her tears.

The plane landed at the airport of Prague. Here it took her two hours of waiting. From here she would fly directly to Madrid. She bought small Coca-Cola and a sandwich, at the same place she ate and again sat down at the waiting room. 45 minutes were left until the plane departure. Passengers sitting in different places seemed to worry. She looked at all of them separately. Then she looked at the man sitting next to her which had the newspaper in his hands. The newspaper was printed in Spanish. After a while the man slowly rose from the chair and passed in front of Lizi limping. Some piece of paper was dropped out from his pocket and could not notice, Lizi got up immediately and ran after him. She called him in English:

- Mister! Mister! The sheet of paper was dropped out of your pocket. Take it – She offered it, but the man ignored it and passed by. Probably for him it was a simple check, or an insignificant paper. Lizi looked at the paper. It was written with well deduced Spanish letters: Lasha Mendoza. She was surprised, whence to a Spanish man an inscription with Georgian name? Why this name, - Lasha - after all it can be her brother and suddenly the good mood surrounded her. If this man sits down in the same plane to Madrid there cannot be any doubt any more. So fast, so simply... Is it real that Lizi will find her brother... She should not loose him from her sight, "After all nothing's happening casually." There must be some kind of connection between this man and my poor brother. This man can be an attorney of my brother. Who knows. That man really got in the plane and tooked a sit right in front of Lizi. Lizi nearly slapped her hands together when she saw him. She looked at the sky through the illuminator with so much pleasure that she felt herself so excellently, as on a ring for karate, when judge loudly enunciate a name of Lizi as the winner's.

Chapter 20

As she took a step on the land of Madrid she felt as if she had spent here all her life. She stood next to the unfamiliar man which was limping on his right feet. The man seemed to be avoiding her sight. Eventually Lizi stopped him on an exit and asked about Madrid. The man negatively shook the head and went to an exit. Lizi looked as limping person went with the accelerated step and felt or it seemed to her that something was connecting her with this man, something main and very important, but all this needed some proofs and facts which could not be found now. The man suddenly disappeared from a view then he appeared again for one moment as he took his sit down in salon of a white "jeep" next to the driver. Lizi in despair hang up a head and went on her way. She already knew the address of the nearest hotel and got on the wagon of a standing tram.

The prices were not so expensive in a small and boring hotel, as they always spoke. She had her light meal and went to her room. And here her nerves was set on edge.. Human weaknesses were proved. What will she do tomorrow or how will she find her brother in this huge city?..

Always so sure that she would definitively find her little brother, here now she was too much hopeless and frightened. Its sentimental humor partially was caused for occurrences of that strange person and as then in the city, when her brother had left the house, in despair started to sob at the top of the voice. For the long-haired administrator guy with an ear-ring it was not remained not noticed occurrence of uncertain orientation of the foreigner in the hotel at one sight, which for similarities to the guy and athletic appearance caused in him some kind of particular interest. For some reason he often came into her room, probably it was the gay and he liked this half girl half boy looking visitor.

At the hotel restaurant table, where Lizi usually sat down, there was the newspaper. Probably someone had left it. Its name was "El Día". Lizi looked through and started to read. And when she finished her dinner, took the newspaper and went to her room. Wished to read it carefully as she strongly decided to find a job in the city what ever it could take. Her pragmatic nature pushed her to this. Empty loss of time couldn't bring her to nowhere. She had to spend all her strength now to find a job. Then it will show a way and a trace... a trace of her lost missed brother.

Suddenly she noticed an announcement which interested her more than others. She attentively read several times, underlined the announcement with a pencil and carefully kept in a small pocket of the bag.

In the evening when Lizi went downstairs to have supper, the the administrator appeared next to her and started the conversation in Spanish. Lizi kept a distance told him that she did not understand his language. And when she finished her dinner got up and went upstairs. He followed the girl with flexible and strange movements of a body, quickly walked upstairs and caught her way at her door. Lizi was very surprised by his behavior, she examined him attentively, the boy embraced her shoulder and started to flirt with her.

Lizi didn't think much, unexpectedly and quickly made few quite movements, put the shameless young man down on the floor and as if nothing had happened entered into her room.

... Just arrived and here it is the trouble what a life?... It can't be done without fight... She thought and touched a hand which apparently had just wounded. By the noise from outside one could tell that probably she had damaged him strongly, but it didn't bother her a lot, because as her intentions and the purposes always were noble on such rudeness she could answer only this way. Absolutely quiet as if nothing had happened she went to bed.

Since then "blue" Robi did not even look at her side, and if some working circumstances impeded him to contact with her he always sent the mate girl.

But her Georgian blood and origin did not give rest to Lizi, for the sake of thirst of struggle for the truth she searched for an occasion to beat him once again...

Chapter 21

Charles returned late from abroad. He asked Flora to bring him a hot cup of coffee and rose upstairs in his room. As he opened the door, he saw a strange picture. Maxi was sleeping next to his bed, having bent his feet and having put a head on forepaws just like a human being. Charles nearly got out of his mind, approached closer and looked at it. On a small bedside table he also saw a medicine. His eyes were widen, took them in his hands and looked... It's Andy's old medicine, why is it here... Since his wife died he has not seen this medicine. During lifetime of Andy she took them five times a day. Suddenly he griped it in an ear, the dog woke up and screeched.

- Maxi - he told angrily.
- What do you want here?..
- Go away at once - Maxi began to bark. Charles looked at it from under the glasses and continued:
- What do you want in my room... –

Maxi looked at it angrily for some time, then as if it was reproaching for something told him with that mystical voice which it only spoke with Lasha at the beginning. Charles noticed a sight of such a close person in his eyes that nearly cried out. Suddenly he shut his eyes by his hands. During this moment Maxi jumped over and faced Flora which walked upstairs. He poured over the hot coffee directly on her and jumped out in the yard. At the same time Flora huddle up from a pain. She had burnt her left cheek and a neck by coffee. They called a doctor at once. Poor woman was crying from the pain all the time. The doctor applied an ointment to her, gave her a medicine and advised her to get some rest. Lasha asked for Max. Max wasn't nowhere, the dog had hidden somewhere like a criminal. At midnight he came back as a thief and laid in his kennel.

Charles decided to train the boy in Spanish and English, he even employed the teacher for this purpose who had to come to him next day. But Lasha knew also other language which wasn't clear to anybody, on which they often spoke with Maxi.

The dog continued to speak with him in that mystical way which wizards used. It was difficult to find out if Lasha was asleep or not. Strange whisper was always audible to him. And so that nobody else could hear it. Nobody could ever guess what was going on between the dog and Charles's new tenant, only in heart of Lasha there was not clear whether it was a fear or an ambiguity. Terrible fear, but subconscious force spoke to him that he should not be afraid of anything that the spirit lodged in the body of the dog wanted only the best for him.

The dog was lying on a sofa like a human being, when the phone rang. It suddenly opened eyes and jump up. Looked around, but when it convinced that there was nobody in the house, went to the phone with wagging the tail. Somehow managed to take the receiver and brought to an ear.

- Hallo! – As if bark was heard in a tube. On other end Charles's voice was heard. Maxi dropped a tube from paws, it tried very hard to take it again but could not. In the end he could take the handset by teeth and put it back. Lasha with widen and scared eyes moved away from the window and climbed in the bad. He was covered up by the blanket and became silent without breathing. He was captured by such a fear that he started to tremble. If only Flora would come and talk to me. Why can't she come to me why?

As he was lying in the bad and he was feeling dog at his feet. He could not move a foot because he felt its fur and was captured by such a horror that he was immovable. He could not even open his eyes. He felt like his eyelids were stuck together and it was lying on his eye-balls with heavy weight. And desire of turning over sideway was so huge that he nearly jumped and ran away. A dog was going on his speeches old way. He was hearing some monotonous voice very close to his ears. That it was like a dream but it was a reality. Each of us at least once in a life had experienced something like that... Something like a thought voice... It was difficult to understand what exactly it was, or who it was... What kind of soul or spirit talked to the boy, as in reality and as in his dreams and sleep...

-Charles is a very good person, trust him. He'll give you everything.

He does not have his own children. Well... So what can one do in such case, he wouldn't kill himself would he? I am now here, probably you can guess who... - the Mystical voice sighed as a human being and continued.

- Flora is a good woman too, but I hate her. Charles did not marry her. When time had come she became his made. She treats me good, but I hate her... And with you she's also kind. Now when you are sleeping she is making a cake for you for tomorrow. All right sleep now I'll go... - The dog moved and jumped off the bed. Lasha sighed with simplification, but he was still shivering.... What did I want here.. Why did I come here at all... I should stay with Bobi? It was all so quiet there and nothing like this would ever occur...

So that's what one get when one goes in vain. Why am I loafing about... Teacher will come tomorrow. After a lesson, I should talk to Flora whether similar voices are audible to her too or not, or whether she notices such kind of strangeness at the dog. Oh! If only I could return to Bobi. Lizi? My beloved little sister?. How is she now?... Has she got used to live without me or not... I should leave to somewhere, I cannot stay here any more... Suddenly the wind moved the curtains, Lasha jumped quickly, closed the window and locked the door by the keys. He sighed with relieve and lay down.

At midnight he felt at feet something with fur and moving again that touched and whispered with him. He also recalled that the door and the window were closed. He sat down on the bad and cried from the top of his voice:

- Lizi, Lizi! - He understood at once that nobody were laying at his feet and that the sensation of a fur was a fear consequence, but the voice, a whispering voice was heard very well, which lulled and sent him into sleep once again.

In the morning as he finished his breakfast and rose upstairs for changing the clothes, as it was cold and the cloudy sky predicted the rain, suddenly he heard Flora calling.

There were two of them in the yard, she and Charles. Charles called the boy to come closer, he told him that he was going out and will be back soon and shook him his big and fat hand again, so as no one could see that he had put in the boy's hand a big amount of money.

At once when he entered back in his room he heard someone calling. Flora with some young lady was rising upstairs. Lasha got lost from this unexpectedness. Flora smiled and said:

- Let me introduce you to your teacher Suzan. -

- The young girl seemed to be twenty two years old, was dressed in a claret dress and long black hair embellished her back. She was hardly smiling to the boy and humbled her head to him:

- Tell me your name please – She said and gave him her hand. Lasha modestly told her his name and led her in his room. Only an hour later Lasha led the teacher to doorway and cheerfully returned in his room. Something new began in his life, more personal, close... Love which promised him a lot of pleasure in the future...

Chapter 22

Lizi took the phone, but to herself she thought: all depends on luck. May be I can find job this way... Who knows... And typed number specified in the announcement containing thirteen digits. She had not to wait for a long, immediately she heard a pleasant female voice that somehow cheered her up. Lizi quickly re-read the announcement text, the woman did not think for a long time, she asked its person and an origin. When she heard the answer, her voice suddenly became strict:

- I don't wish the foreigner nurses – She told and hanged up. It had afflicted Lizi, but she did not consider this first failure for the misfortune.

At the same time she passed to the text of other announcement. This one was for the nurse searched for the four-year child, for English-speaking young girl. Lizi thought that her fortune can smile to her this time. She obeyed to an internal voice. Her honest nature and practice received by education of her little brother, necessarily would serve a really good job to her on a post of the nurse... As the tutor she can give a pleasant impression and will work honesty indeed. She dialed the number at once. She heard a man's voice that a little bit confused her, but she gathered all forces and began conversation in perfect English. This time no one asked about her origin, the man seemed to be very polite interlocutor, gave his address and asked to come in the morning as then a family could have left to somewhere on a visit.

Lizi has started to prepare herself at once, she found all necessary documents, translated into English and Spanish languages. As a multiple winner of Karateka, she had all awards with her, put everything in her bag and reconsidered the address.

"What should I where?" Now she started to think about her appearance, looked at the jeans fitting her body. I have to buy a dress for me. The dress is important. She said and started to prepare in a rush; took a small purse and went out. She started to look around and searched, but there were no shops nearby, she didn't even think to ask someone about where she could find a shop, she was quite sure that she could find it herself, at a crossroads curtailed in left. In several meters the big shop appeared, from outside abreast clothes demonstrated was visible. Allocated with set and a variety... She didn't have to go anywhere else she could buy anything here she walked upstairs quickly and entered the shop. Passed on a number of clothes then on the second row the choice was huge. She did not know what style would fit her better because as long as she remembered herself, she never wore a dress. She looked all over for a while and suddenly stopped.

Sympathetic girl appeared from somewhere who smiled at her courteously and asked:

- Can I help you Miss? -

Lizi's face shined with a sudden smile. The question returned her in a far past, she recalled Tbilisi shop of the mixed goods and money from the first salary. With money, that she had bought the wig of her dream, being still a little girl. The smiling and surprised face of Georgian woman faced her.... She could not start talking for a while... Suddenly loudly and sincerely laughed:

- Thanks! I will choose myself - She told and took a dark blue dress from the hanger.

Lizi in a dress (if someone would see her in Georgia one would faint from surprise...) It was so strange, as if imagining the king of Spain Juan Carlos in the Georgian national clothes named "Chokha-Akhaluhi" in the centre of Madrid, in 1975.

Dress which she had never worn before, now became clothes of her dream. As if by buying a dress something extraordinary had to happen, she opened a door in some absolutely new and successful future... She tried on that one and another, eventually she removed thin violet jeans dress, one piece suite and quickly as if she were in a hurry, went to dressing room. She quickly changed clothes; turned and told to herself in a mirror:

- It is delightful – She gave a sign to shop girl from the far to make her come to her... Shop girl beautifully wrapped the dress to her, put it in a bag; drew the check and said goodbye. Lizi went further.

Now naturally she had to buy high-heeled shoes. There were many people in the shoes section. She looked at shoes with average heels, dressed and walked, she had never stood on high heels before, she started staggering. She was pumped over that in left than in the right. In a moment it seemed to her she was very ridiculous and she burst out laughing. "It's OK I will get used to it" she said in the end and called the saleswoman. Then she passed in perfumery section... Here she chose perfume and petty things. She bought beautiful watches and silver brooch. Fool with happiness once again looked back around and left shop gracefully.

In the hotel room she changed her clothes again and put on a dress one piece suite. Looking in the mirror she did not laugh any more. The beautiful girl looked at her from there with a big grey eyes and a high forehead. With the direct refined lines... With a small lovely nose which seemed just grown, appeared very differently... She let her hair fall down and also started very unusual business for her, a make-up. Could not make up an eye, it was smeared and she had to wash the face several times. Eventually she decided to put on a make-up simply sunburn powder and violet lipstick on her lips.

On the specified address came an incredible girl. Young man opened the door. As soon as Lizi stepped on the threshold she thought that her destiny brought her in the best place. The smile appeared on her lips and it made her accurate and expressed features more beautiful.

Her eyes sparkled in lighted bulbs of the hall, she shined out so much beauty that it seemed that she illuminated all hall. Heart of Lizi answered definitively all not clear questions and she looked into the man's face fool with the confidence.

The man examined the girl from head to her foot, and he did not try to hide an admiration. On the contrary, stepped for measures of decency and met the guest with compliments. He pointed to sit down on fancy armchair and he himself fell in an armchair nearby. Suddenly the child appeared from somewhere, first he looked at daddy, then at the guest as if making a choice. At last went to Lizi and nestled on her as to the old acquainted and to the favorite person. The man smiled happily that meant that from this day his only child and the new acquainted should live together - in Mr. Navarro's family.

Chapter 23

In the afternoon Flora put clothes of Lasha in washing machine and went to the court yard with a basket in hands.

- I'm going shopping - She told to herself than to anyone else and looked towards Lash's room. Lasha's teacher was already there. Flora heard their conversation or study from far and with some happy sensation left the house.

That evening Flora tried fall asleep early. Charles came back home late too. Lasha was studying in his room till late at night. It was about midnight when the dog having risen his ears and started to walk between rooms. Obviously it was disturbed. Suddenly it approached to Flora's room and opened the door by a nose. Flora slept with a deep sleep. Max stopped at her room and squealed... Looked at the sleeper, it had such a look as if wished to eat the slipping woman alive.

After a while it passed next to the Charles' room and stopped at the bathroom. By the same way it pushed the door with the nose but a door was densely closed. In the end it snapped at the handle and turned it downwards. The door creaked and opened.

It approached to washing machine. It tried to open washing machine door by forelegs. This attempt resulted to be more difficult. But it did not surrender and tried to open it anyway. Eventually it opened some how. It put his nose directly into washing machine. It caught Lasha's trousers by teeth and accurately without touching a floor put them on his back and went to terrace. Put semi wet trousers on a dryer standing on a terrace and returned to washing machine again. In the same way it took out shirts and underwear, put them on a dryer too and passed by the house from the back side, jumped in a window and came to the head of Lasha's bed.

It was clear that Lasha slept very strong. He didn't hear anything. Max rose on forelegs at the bed. He looked at him for a while, then jumped on the bed, picked up a pose for a dream, put a head on his feet and fell asleep.

In the morning when Flora entered the bathroom, saw that the washing machine door was open. Somebody had already taken out all clothes at the dryer. How could I forget? Ashamed she closed the door and went out. Is it possible that Lasha took care of clothes...Quickly went out on a terrace. Sees things suspended in such disorder... Even most clumsy person could not hang them in such disorder... She went to a Lasha's room, Lasha denied, told that he doesn't know anything. Then Flora approached to Charles's room. Charles was not there. It is excluded that Charles would have touched clothes at all... Then who? Who opened the washing machine door; who took out things on a terrace; who took care of clothes of the boy if not him... Yes him... Flora shook a head and looked aside to Maxes kennel.

When Charles returned home he brought two tickets for a football match. Called Lasha and asked:

- Lasha! Tomorrow "Real" Madrid on the home field accepts "Manchester United", do you like football?

Lasha suddenly grew pale. He couldn't say a word for a while... Football?.. of course he loves football. Even more he's crazy about it, He spent his childhood dreaming of it... Finally he had started to train... Started but so what... He trained only for five months... Eh... It didn't worth it. He waved his hand and looked at Charles in the eyes. Charles repeated his question loudly:

- Do you like football boy?

- I love it, certainly. - He answered the boy.

- Then get ready. We are expected to see good game - Lasha was delighted, with gratefulness looked at Charles. The boy as always has became now on a good mood from eternally presence of Charles benevolence. At the same moment went to his room and after a while returned with a photo camera in his hands. It's been a long time since he did not make pictures of anything, the passion has passed? No. This can't be truth. He simply doesn't have much time... The Spanish and English lessons and even more their fine teacher forced him to forget about all. About the childhood itself and about the story that caused him living on a foreign territory. It is necessary to have a free time, for traveling and taking pictures.

Suddenly he looked at old photos. He noticed a photo of sleeping Lizi "My Lizi" he spoke silently and tears appeared on his eyes.

Memories about Georgia faced to his eyes: Tbilisi house, School, Lizi,... Her eternal care and protection.

Park "Sam"... How Lizi had beaten boys... "My favourite sister" here he suddenly smiled. But quite fast such a melancholy embraced him again. Such a torture that each second became for him suffering. He took a sit right there next on the floor; buried his head in his hands. Suddenly he heard Flora calling, called for a dinner. The boy thanked and so that nobody could notice his tears, turned on back to the house and went to the kennel of the dog.

Max looked at the boy with sympathy. As if it noticed his grief, approached closer. Put forepaws on his shoulders, and as much as dog could do caressed him. Lasha also snuggled his head. But mentally he was far away somewhere else. He was watching the sky and was repeating to the dog or to someone else the same phrase:

"My God show me my Lizi!... My Lizi... My sweet Liz..." Suddenly he got angry... He looked at the dog: "I never had a mother, why is it that everybody wants to be my mother. Leave me alone" he cried and ran to his room; stuck a head into a pillow and began to cry just like than when on the second day after funeral of his mother, when instead of mother four years old child was woken by his aunt, when he did not want anybody and anything else but his own mother. The nineteen years old proud boy cried, cried a river… an orphanhood and melancholy on the sister... And Max itself whom now in the different ways, as a dog and as human has vested on him cargo of being son irritated him. Pity and anger simultaneously melancholy embraced him and he sighted as if it took away his heart.

Crying and tears brought him some calm and he felt asleep. Flora in vain called him for a dinner. The boy slept sound sleep. Only in the evening he was woken up in absolute quietness. Took his camera again and left for the court yard. The dog was lying asleep. Lasha clicked the camera directly under his ear. Max pricked up his ears. Suddenly he became gay, passed by the court yard jumping up. Laha ran behind it on heels and photographed it. Unexpectedly the dog pricked up ears and directed the look towards Lasha. Lasha shuddered; he faced a strange sight... As he thought he saw this sight before... And that in the nearest past... Interestingly where?.

He strained trying to recall, but still does not recollect. Who can it be, to whom Max is similar. Whose face is it eventually, suddenly he left the dog and ran in Charles' room. He took a look at Andy's photo in a frame on the table. Charles's deceased wife was looking at him from the frame, just as Max from the photo camera screen. Strong similarity frightened him. He quickly closed the door and went to see Charles.

Charles started to speak with him about football again. The boy half-heartedly answered his questions. He was surprised that Charles did not see this obvious strangeness in the house. The strangeness and similarity. Not similarity but a revived soul of his wife in the body of Max. He does not want to stay in this house any more. What a strange things occur here... He should rise and leave this place. But... It would be ingratitude, but also he does not want to stay any more. Unique person with whom it is heavy for him to say goodbye is his charming teacher. Hard is not the word. Love sneaked up to his heart, as fragile and charming as Suzan herself, gentle and sensitive. Indescribable, Lasha rose in his room, decided to leave in a short term. It's still early for preparing. He looked at books and note-books on the table.

Suddenly beautiful Suzan appeared in front of his eyes and suddenly a smile lighted up his face. Tomorrow when Suzan comes he'll tell her that he loves her and is not going to live without her. Probably Suzan will tell the same. Lasha feels it, the celebratory sight of the girl speaks to him about this... And this feeling compels him to stay here, in the Charles's house at least while all will clear up.

Chapter 24

Lasha is already twenty years old. Tall, dark brown hair and eyes. Short beard gives him a strict and courageous image, the beard suits very well to his face.

The teacher started to come more often. She came twice a week to the nice foreigner but she comes now three and four times a week. It's obvious that force of love pulls her back to the Mendoza family. And Lasha in a perfectly tidy condition is in expectation of Suzan all day long.

Nobody can tell obviously or secretly but he's in love with all his heart and soul. And for expression of love he considers that the ideal way is to drill his lessons. Learns languages with the big eagerness and looks on road from a window. Minutes spent together with her studying are given also to love and in viewing each other and in this way time runs pleasantly and imperceptibly.

On Sunday Lasha invited Suzan for a walk in the city. He told that he wishes to make some pictures... They walked in city and even had got a bit tired. Laughed and had a fun... Laha took the pictures of the girl, in the end they sat down in cozy cafe where Lasha made a declaration of love to her. Suzan embraced the boy strongly, with pleasure informed him that she had fallen in love for the first time and that had only read in the books about such a strong feelings. They have spent together all evening, then Lasha saw her off at the house. On way he bought to her the big bunch of flowers and repeated to her words of love. Infinitely happy Suzan did not want to go home. She passionately kissed the boy. The Loving couple would not like to get apart. It was so hard for astounded couple to get apart, they decided to spend night on suburb to find some cozy place, (as they considered), original lovers should make also a big fire and have a sleep on a grass too.

Charles looked at watches it was one o'clock in the morning. He silently approached to the room of Flora and called her:

- Where should we search the boy? -

- He must be with Suzan in a city - She answered sleeping Flora.

- With Suzan?... Why... What's an occasion? -

- You know Charles!... In my opinion they love each other... I think so... -

Charles fell thinking a little:

- Well, in this case there is nothing bad... - He calmed down a little - Where can they be now?...

- I don't know anything, Lasha is the big boy, and clever as well. Do not grieve Charles! Sleep... –

- He left his cell phone at home -

- Where's the dog? - Suddenly Flora recalled Max.

- It doesn't shows up neither. - Charles looked round the court yard.

- The poor thing probably searches for him - Flora said.

- Should I call the police? -

- No Charles... Don't do that... I'm sure everything is all right with them. -

- All right I'll go. Good night! -

- Sweet dreams... - Flora replaced a side, but now she became restless. Tossed in the bed tossed, eventually got up, put on a dressing gown and went to look in the court yard. Max had returned, was lying on its place, and gnawed the forepaws.

Having returned early morning Lasha had great pleasure from the taken bath, and then fell asleep strongly.

Later Charles and Flora found him sleeping in his room and it made them very much delighted but Max also fell asleep in the usual pose at feet of Lasha, and blood flew from his paws.

In the evening Charles and Flora approached to standing Lasha on the terrace. None of them dared to ask him about last night. Lasha looked happily at his virtuous people. He was ready to answer all their questions. To speak about Suzan, it was a huge pleasure for him now, but any of them didn't say a word. They started a conversation about Max.

After a while Charles apologized and went to get some rest, Flora went to prepare the dinner, Lasha also wanted to get alone and to think of beautiful Suzan, but Max never gave him a rest... The strange behavior, he demanded an attention to itself all the time. Lahsa went to his room.

Charles from the terrace of his room, Flora from a small window of the kitchen, and Lasha from an open door, secretly from each other, for the same reason, observed Max. All three perfectly knew, but could not confess to each other that Max's so-called body possessed soul of person well familiar to the family. The soul which had shown herself only after Lasha appeared in this house, the soul of infertile woman accepted and loved Lasha as her own son, and observed her husband as the jealous wife just like she always did while she was alive, especially when Charles was living the house tidy.

Max stretched and lay down in the court yard. Put forepaws under a head, closed eyes and fell asleep just like Charles' dead wife did, having her feet bent like when she had pain in her stomach. Charles and Flora had noticed the familiar pose at once and in fright quickly closed doors.

Lasha had never seen Andy before, so he didn't notice anything surprising. Max wasn't only a dog any more it was very close friend who wanted only kindness and happiness for him...

In the morning Charles took Flora with him and went somewhere. Before leaving Max turned around the car for a long time, barked on them, ran in back than in front of the car. When Charles left, Max entered his room, found the TV switched on, then switched it off by blowing paws on the remote control. Then it snatched Charles's bed sheets by teeth and dragged it on the floor. He tormented all bed sheets with his teeth. Suddenly he snatched Andy's photo by teeth which was at Charles's bed's head on a small locker. It snatched, threw photo on the floor by teeth and started to beat it by four paws. It trampled it before it got broken. Then he approached to Lasha's room's window and as if it started to call the sleeping boy, it told to him something of two syllables. Probably in its own language told "Lasha"... What else could Andy's soul tell to the desired son.

At Midday Charles appeared on the road. He was driving, and Flora's brown hair was seen nearby. When they stopped at the house, Charles gave something to Flora. Flora did not even have a chance to leave the car as the dog had jumped in her way, snatched a teeth to her dress and pulled so hard that it stripped her a half of it.

Woman screamed, Max snatched now a second half. Lasha immediately ran up to her, tried to take it in hands, but it was so embittered, that didn't even admitted the boy nearby. Barked and growled until it hadn't torn also other half of dress and only after that it went away. Woman stood among the court yard totally naked and dishonored and tried to cover naked body with scraps of the torn clothes and continued to cry with despair.

Charles called Lasha. Now the dog turned to him. Also cut his way. Began to bark at him once or twice, snatched his trousers and pulled them down too. Charles suddenly grasped his head. His departed wife was looking at him by the dog's eyes, embittered and splashing out the anger. Charles couldn't stand this expression, quickly entered the room and locked the door after him. Here he was expected by not less terrible picture. His bed sheets were rolled on the floor, burst in shreds, and framed picture of Andy and himself was burst in small pieces by someone (now it's quite clear by who or what).

Chapter 25

Two weeks had passed. Charles left every morning somewhere, as if for arranging some affairs. Lasha and his beautiful teacher passed lessons of foreign languages and love as well and they were madly happy. Max as guilty and punished, was adhered all the time. Proceeding from it, Flora felt safe too. Only Lasha used to come to her, bringing him a meal. And sometimes he sat down nearby and looked at him. Probably he was sorry for the animal... The Animal or... He could not make out was it what or who... And sometimes he had desire to tell her about his childhood, about the orphanhood, about the little sister, to tell something about Bobi and Suzan... Why exactly to Max... Why not to Flora or Charles, or Suzan, It was exactly in what Lasha could not make out.

Lahsa stroked the dog on the head, looked him in the eyes with compassion and said:

- Max, don't you want to make peace with Flora, With Charles? - Suddenly Max let out the strange voice from his throat and tears began to flow from her eyes, Max cried, cried bitterly, as if she was the person. With all her heart and was embracing Lasha. Charles smoked a cigarette and called Flora.

Flora what is it happening upon us - Flora was all trembling.

- What do you think, is it her? He asked Charles again after a while...

- I do not think, I know for sure... She behaved the same way... -

- I felt it, I knew... - Hardly could Charles speak up.

- She hates me, she's jealous - Flora began to cry. Got the handkerchief from a pocket and covered her eyes with it.

- She loves only Lasha in this house. Loves him as the son – Hardly could Charles speak up.

- Yes, she loves him. All she had ever dreamed of was her own child in her life. Of course she will love him... – Flora dropped her head down.

- How many times I saw her jumping out from his windows. She sleeps with him at night.

- All went wrong, when I just started a new life. - Charles sighed. –He had found the remarkable boy, planned on the future. -

Suddenly they had seen Max gently embracing the boy on shoulders and got quiet and calm image. Lasha bent to his ear and whispered him something. At first Max spent his eyes all around then looked at Lasha and nodded. Charles looked at Flora, both felt that they made common cause.

- Flora had a presentiment that a strange story had established in this house, by all means it had something in common with spirits and outer space forces existing in spirits and was frightened very much.

Lasha went to Charles.

- Come here please - Charles voice was trembling.

- What do you think Lasha, who it is? -

Lasha dropped his head, his large and beautiful forehead was covered by sweat. His eyebrows were frown. He was rubbing his long refine fingers and was taking his time before giving him an answer ... Charles repeated his question, he deeply sighed, looked paternal directly in his eyes and said:

- If I got it right it's your wife - Charles and Flora looked at each other and told simultaneously:

- We think so too -

- As I have noticed she looks at me as her son. It is too hard for me as I had never had a mother... As long as I have remember myself... Lasha indulged in memories...

- From the date of my arrival I feel that she treats me very strangely. Even if she's a dog and cannot make for me sandwiches as Flora - Lasha tried to amuse them and looked at Flora.

- We should get rid of it –Charles said.

- How is it possible? - The boy was indignant – it's the same if we turn out one of our family members -

- And what shall we do then son! -

- You should get used to her and do not forget she's your wife...
- Lasha put excessive severity in his words, he believed that he was

only one who could resolve this difficult and not clear situation in the family.

- You can't give her away not sell, neither kill her... You should love her, she's a person... And still... - Here Lasha stopped for a minute:

- She wants to apologize to you both. - Hardly could he say in the end.

They looked at each other surprised, then they darted a glance at Lasha. Both expressed the consent silence. Lasha approached to the dog, took the collar off and - called her to go with him - Max calmed first at Flora's and then at Charles' feet. She was with dropped head for a long time and then rubbed the body about them that meant that since this day enmity between them has ended.

- Well, I should go to sleep. Good night! - Said amazed Charles and passed by three of them.

Chapter 26

Lizi now had already got herself busy in the new job, imposed in performing her duties so much, that she sometimes forgot why she had arrived in Madrid at all. Though education of this lovely and little boy was returning her in the past and reminding her childhood time after time, an orphaned life and the little brother for whom she had arrived. In the morning she and little boy Toni went out for a walk in a garden, then at breakfast time came back home. The boy was in the age in which her little brother was orphaned. This kid doesn't have mum too. It is completely assigned a role of mother to Lizi also here. Suddenly tears appeared in Lizi's eyes:

- Lash, I miss you so much, my brother!... - Tears as a streamlet poured down from her eyes. As then, now also it seems to her that only Lasha was orphaned that only parents of Lasha were past away instead of hers... The Poor girl always forgot about herself for her brother's sake. She never had her own life neither had experienced not misfortune nor happiness.

Anyhow, the past with its stories and events again rose in Lizi's life. Small Toni resulted to be very lovely. The main thing is that he loved his nurse very much and Lizi as a small and fragile creation treated him with special care.

On one Sunday morning Lizi took tiny Toni for a walk in the park, she took the large infant book with drawings with them when they sat down on the chair, the child could not calm down. He persistently asked to go to the shop. Lizi took him away from park and stopped at the shop entrance. Suddenly at cash desk she saw familiar lame man whom she had seen at the airport in Prague which had dropped a piece of paper and with whom despite the big desire couldn't achieve to get acquainted. She decided to approach him now at least more close and not to miss the chance to get known him. She ran up to the policeman standing at the corner:

- She asked him to watch over the child for a minute, I'll be back at once... – She said it quickly and ran to the shop never looking back.

She took a big packet of pop corn from a shelf and approached to cash desk, rose nearby and looked him right in the face. The man did not her any attention at all, with purchases in his hands went to the doors. Lizi ran after him. Suddenly (as though) he stroke with him and fell down; fell down directly to lame sick foot of man and started to cry. Naturally it was very painful for the stranger, but he never minded of himself. He bent over fallen girl, took her by the hand and helped her to rise. He called people for the aid. Lizi pretended that she had a pain in her foot and continued to cry.

Until the doctor was not called the stranger hadn't moved away not for a step from the girl. And then he disappeared. Lizi looked back when she was convinced that the man had disappeared without the trace, Lizi rose, became straight, thanked to everybody presented there for help and went away from the shop. Only now she recalled the child. Suddenly she got worried. She started to look around. Having looked at an opposite side, she saw the policeman holding the child by the hand and walked around before a photo gallery.

Lizi ran up to the child. "Apologized for what had happeneded" and suggested some pop corn first to him then to the child. The policeman smiled. thanked and returned to his place. Lizi continued her way together with the child. "... Thank God I have not thrown the child on an arbitrariness... he would get lost it's obvious, What would I do then?" Thinking it over Lizi began to tremble for fear.

Suddenly she noticed the advertising. She approached closer. She read the text concerning the opening of photo-exhibition. "This huge building will contain myriads of visitors... I will come and I will look around. If I am not mistaken the photo competition will take its place here."

Lizi was very much pleased by this information. She decided to come to gallery what ever it takes on September 28-29. But before that she has to find out about the lame person. Should learn about him some more what ever it takes... That's her decision. Mysterious communication which exists between them is surrounded by some secret. If she can't find out herself, Lizi will necessarily ask the father of the child for help. As well she will tell the reason of her arrival in Madrid. She deeply believes that he will help her to find this strange mysterious person.

Chapter 27

Streets of Tbilisi are covered by yellow and red leaves of autumn. A wind song is heard from the windows and a cold is getting stronger and stronger at night.

Man wrapped up in black clothes, walks in the "Vake" cemetery. It's evening. The wind here is swept more, than on the central streets of the city. Some minutes earlier here and there were audible cry which had just stopped. It had stopped because it darkened and people went home. The man noticed a white marble stone from far away. His recently departed wife is buried here. He had stopped.

He doesn't hurry up to approach more close. He suddenly started to howl as a wolf. He looked back on fossilized cemeteries. All is as one for him now. He began to cry for everybody with one fate then turned to his one. Has sat down absolutely close to a marble stone, lighted a match and shined the area. Tika's face looked straight into his eyes. He approached closer, leant lips and kissed the marble. "How cold are you" told her and passed his hand on her face. Suddenly he turned away and went down on the road downwards.

"Tika, my girl... why did you leave me..." – He said and took a gulp of vodka at a small booth round the corner. It seemed he wasn't so cold any more. He checked if his keys were in his pocket "here it is" and he went on walking further. As he entered home he sighted bottles scattered on the floor. He drinks three months without a stop.

He entered the room staggering. At the mirror he saw Tika's favorite perfume "Christian Dior"... And there was the toy car wallowed on the floor. The car which he decided to buy when he saw the father and son walking down the street. The child strong held the toy and the father strong held the son by the hand and they both happy went along the street. Later Nika carried out the dream, he bought the toy car too, bought when he married Tika. When the pleasure of expectation of the son was warming his heart, but what... Nika grabbed the toy, pressed it to his heart and began to cry a river.

- No my son! I could not become worth of you. I could not achieve to become the father. Mum left and took you with her... – He leant against the wall with his back and fell on the floor. After a while he fell deep asleep hugging the toy to his heart.

In the morning Nika woke up on the floor. He was ashamed. He was ashamed of himself and rose up quickly. He recalled how boring life was, emptiness and loneliness to him before. He recall the years of searching and hopelessness... And that night, that nightmare, that he associated with the hell... Then he was angry with this world without any reason. But now... Now he's got real reason. Some reason he's got. Tika's gone... She's gone forever...

Suddenly he turned to the wall and stroked the mirror. Huge mirror fell apart with murmur. The noise or anger made clear the boy's mind... It seemed that sorrow went away too. He bent over and started to gather the fragments of broken mirror. He gathered one by one as if this action gave him a pleasure. After a while he sat on the sofa. He recalled Lizi... And suddenly he got up.

He decided to handle with his sorrow and to begin a new life. He rose up, firstly he tidied up home, took out the bottles, swept the floors. He put a candle at Saint George's icon, eventually he swore that he would stop drinking and would not turn his back to the life. "I have to know how Lizi is, it's been already more than a year as I know nothing about her". I will visit her cousin sisters and I will ask them about Lizi. Nika entered the bathroom, shaved and beautifully dressed left the house.

Nika came back home with very pleasant news. Small and fragile Ani, after heart operation, she totally recovered, married the most well-known architect of the city and already had given birth to two children. And Tika was still waiting for her destiny and lived with her mother. As to orphans, the brother and sister, their history filled Nika's heart with pleasure. Lizi worked in a fine family as the nurse and according to Tika's words she had found a trace of her little brother. After a while they possibly would arrive in Georgia and will stay here. For Nika it was delightful to hear all this. Nika widely opened windows and deeply inhaled cool air of autumn. He felt that love of Lizi, the childhood and cloudless youth as if a fresh flower still lived inside of him.

Chapter 28

Charles found out the information about Lasha's passion for photography lately. He took a glance at his photos, he was very happy. Especially the landscapes of Georgia impressed him. Churches and villages located at tops of mountains. Suddenly he looked him right at his face and asked:

- You had such a motherland, what have you forgotten abroad? - Lasha preferred to keep silence. He didn't answer him at all. Melancholy covered his face that didn't remain without Charles notice.

- All right, don't speak... The Main thing is that you're here... For me it is remarkable. - Lasha was still quiet.

- Take the car, here you'll also find remarkable places. -

The next day Charles bought the best camera for him . Lasha was very much delighted. In the same evening he left the house. For the second day he left again, he took and took photos. Charles showed him sights. And then took the boy in the Madrid museum. Lasha could not hide admiration.

In one of those evenings Charles informed Lasha that in two days he would take a part in photo competition. Together with pictures made in the childhood in Georgia, he asked him to prepare the Madrid photographic material for a competitive exhibition too.

The building of a photo gallery could not feet in visitors. Building walls divided into three halls were overloaded by photos. The ground floor building was occupied completely with people entering from streets. Charles and Lasha stood in one corner of the right wall and watched people. One aged man approached to Charles. Charles was very much delighted to meet him. He called Lasha and introduced to him. Then they walked aside and started to talk. The stranger occasionally secretly glanced at Lasha. And he nodded to Charles all the time. Soon they had agreed about something and squared up. Charles approached to Lasha and as if he was sharing a secret with him he whispered in his ear:

- He's my lawyer. I asked him to put in order my documents, you should be there too - Lasha was surprised, but he didn't say anything. He nodded him in agreement and started to look over as if looking for someone.

Suzan appeared in the doorway. Gentle and charming. She wore white dress which transparent collar hanged down from her shoulders in all length. And her chestnut-coloured curly hair was sparkling in all length. At her sight Lasha got smitten by love, quickly moved off his place and went to meet her. Took her for a hand and brought to Charles:

- Mister Charles! let me introduce my bride to you - All of them smiled simultaneously. Charles gave a hand to the girl:

I'm very pleased to meet you. You are right Lasha, I'll shake this girl's hand for the first time as to your bride - Charles hadn't yet seen happy smile of Lasha. He embraced him as his own son and congratulated.

- Lasha took Suzan's arm and led her to the photos. Charles sent both with a smile, took his inseparable cane and started to view photos.

Lizi and Edward stepped out of the car. They stopped in front of the gallery. Then they entered into open door and went on top of a long stairs. Wide walls of the high building were full of pictures. Suddenly Lizi saw beautiful Suzan going opposite. Suzan was so dazzling; she accidentally smiled having seen her. Then she looked on nearby standing boy. The boy went nearby hanging a head holding her by arm.

- What a familiar face? – Lizi persistently looked at the boy. The boy walked on by her, he also turned a head back, he looked at her not with a less amazed expression.

- She looks like Lizi so much, But hey!...What can be Lizi doing here? - The boy decided and looked away at once.

- Whence I know him?... Who is he?... – Lizi started to walk slowly. Then they mixed up with the others. They lost each other, but Lizi continued to search for that beautiful girl and the boy with a beard going nearby. "Where has she seen this boy with the beard?" she tries to remember but can't recall. The boy looked around too, at the same time he was afraid that Suzan could notice his persistent searching of someone....

The hall slowly became empty. Suddenly Lizi saw that lame man in front of Gallery, which she had seen first in Prague and then at cash desk in shop several days before. She stood at the right door of the white jeep and looked somewhere in the distance getting on his toes as if he was searching for someone. Lizi became agitated. She absolutely lost a head... She did not take away an eye of him. Edward was speaking to her but she couldn't hear anything.

Suddenly that beautiful person which she had just been seen by Lizi with the bearded guy approached to the lame man. She told him something and turned at the doors site. Lizi looked towards the doors too. Now from the far distance she could make out a profile of the boy with a beard very well. Paparazzi had stopped him at an exit and asked him about something perseveringly. Suddenly someone came forward with the big photo in hands and announced:

- The photo competition is over. See the photo work of the winner and lifted the photo up and showed up it to the people.

Lizi rose on her toes. She pulled forward; she almost transferred nearly on top of the crowd. She looked at the lifted photo. My God! It's her. Lizi...Who made this photo... When... When was it taken... She sleeps on the bed, holding a magazine in her hand and from under the thin blanket half naked back is seen.

Suddenly she understood everything. It got darkened in her eyes, she nearly fell down. Reporters loudly called for Lasha Mendoza. Lizi already recognized her brother. She broke through a wave of people as a swimmer in the sea, with tears on her cheeks she ran forward. She saw a back of Lasha and reached her hand and touched his back. Lasha turned around, suddenly he appeared opposite to her. He recognized her sister too, by her smile and her eyes, recognized and embraced her... "My Liz" he said and strongly embraced her in his heart.

Chapter 29

Lasha took a look at Bobi's house. He came here with Charles because he decided to see Bobi. He ran down the stairs quickly, he told Charles that would be back soon and went on his way fast. He got some rest near the house. He's heart was beating hard. He pushed a bell button and stood stained and breathless.

No one opened a door. He looked around. He rang a bell button again. He suddenly called without thinking:

- Bobi! – Agitation appeared in his voice. Unusual silence last too long. As if his heart predicted, Bobi shouldn't be at home. Not only at home but at the territory of Madrid at all... He suddenly saw an old man which came out on a balcony, he held a knife in his hand and was peeling some fruit with a shaking hand. Lasha bowed to him:

- Excuse me... Bobi lived here. Could you tell me... Bobi a young boy...

- He's gone – The old man waved a hand.

- Doesn't he live here any more? – The boy asked sadly. The man looked at him with displeasure, didn't tell him anything, showed him a back and entered the house.

... Where could he be gone?.. The boy mumbled and looked towards Charles gardens. The sun stood on the edge of the sky and was sending a goodbye smile to the earth. It was shown on Lasha's gloomy face that he had no any desire to stay here. He went on his way as a tired passenger.

Charles took him by hand, told him that he planned to show him everything around here and let him to backyard. He took him all over the place, he even showed him a secret safe and finally as if no one could hear him whispered something in his ear.

Lasha was on a bad mood but he was nodding politely and humbly anyway. Charles didn't feel his bad humor. He was telling him something and leading him forward. Lasha was still having heavy thoughts about Bobi "He must have returned to England and had taken Janita with him..."

In the evening they got in a car, Lasha fit the keys and rushed on the route as fast as he could. They rode silently to the house. The silence of Chares amazed the boy but he never asked a thing.

Flora met them at the doorway. She held some kind of invitation card and was looking with a smile to their faces. Charles didn't even look at Flora. He grew pale and hardly could breath. Flora ran to him, took him by his arm and asked:

- Charles! Are you all right!.. – Charles didn't say a word. They made him lie down in the room and opened windows widely. In some minutes he fell asleep. Flora looked at him sleeping for several times along the night. She entered the room quietly on her toes and listened to his rapid respiration.

In the morning Charles got up early. He ate a yogurt and a piece of cake. Then he sat down on the terrace, Max lay to his feet, it didn't move until Charles had gone to lie down.

That night Max's behavior was quite strange. It was running up and down. It was howling. Lasha was asking him to calm down but the dog was standing on his guns. The boy felt the expected misfortune. The story or myth he had heard in his childhood that howl of the dog was the prediction sign of the death.

At the midnight Flora ran into Lasha's room.

- Get up for the God's sake, Charles feels badly - She stood right on the sleepy boy and cried over his head. Lasha got up at once. He quickly got dressed and followed her. Charles was sitting on his bed and hardly could breath:

- Come over... I'm too bed my son! – He spoke curtly. Lasha held his shoulders; he looked in his eyes pityingly.

- Don't look at me with such a scare... I'm your father... –

- Everything you see here is yours... And there too... – Charles signed him by his eyes in the direction of the suburb.

- I have got a house in Prague...-And after a while he continued:

-Don't leave me boy... I don't have anybody but you... –

- Don't worry I'll call the doctor – Lasha left his hand and ran to the phone. Flora made him swallow another couple of pills again. Charles now looked in her eyes and asked:

- Flora! My Florita! This is my boy. Don't leave him. Be to him as loyal as you were to me... – Charles suddenly turned up his eyes and fell on the bed. Lasha saw how the death slept inside through the open door, how he grubbed the man's hand and how he pushed him to fall on the bed. And Flora saw a steam coming out of his mouth, gray soul sparkling out of him upwards and mixed with the ear.

Max was standing in the doorway, as someone close of the deceased and mourning and it was a pity to look at him... As someone guilty he had dropped his head down towards the flour and was crying a river.

Lasha called Lizi at once

- Come, I need you - ... Lizi appeared to his house in half an hour. She looked at Charles and said:

- I know him... – Lasha didn't asked how. He asked Flora to make a coffee for her, and he himself went to the undertaker's office.

Charles was buried properly. Everybody returned into the house. But Max remained on the cemetery. Lately he came back home.

Lizi looked around the house. She didn't ask to tell anything, she understood everything herself. She got closer to her brother and held him as in old times. Both of them felt the familiar warmness, distant and their own, something only they could understand and familiar only for them... Lasha felt Lizi's care again... He recalled his orphan, hopeful years... And there at the land of Madrid, even Endy's soul that ruled a dogs body was congratulating truly by barking but with all her heart the great joy produced by encountering the sister and brother eventually that have been lost for each other for such a long time, and had tasted a bitterness of an orphanage.

Chapter 30

Nika counted the money. "Twenty five thousand dollars? What is this... Who is sending so much money to him?" Bank employee also noticed confusion and surprise. She asked him with comparison "if he felt all right?". Then suggested him to take a sit on a chair. Nika's hands were trembling; he hardly signed the check and took a sit on the chair.

He took a look on a sheet. Some Lasha Mendoza was sending him the money. Who can it be... what money is this and why is he sending them to him. Thoughts carried him away in a far past.

"So what brother? You'll return it back when you'll grow up..." he recalled his words, also the day when Lasha called him. The boy was too scared and pale.

- Ani's too bad – He said and tears had come out in the boy's eyes. What could Nika do... He visited one by one the block boys, asked money from every one. At list he could do this favor to orphan kids. He found money for them to save their cousin. Nika looked at the check again, smiled and stood up quickly. He went out the door and looked at the sparkling from the sunshine sky hopefully.

Lizi was doing her gym in the yard on the carpet. She was as athletic and strong as she was in Lasha's childhood. She was wearing the boy's wig on her head, the one she had bought by her first salary in the childhood there in Tbilisi. Lizi especially dressed up in athletic and old way, to show herself to little brother strong end winner once again...

To remind him home, Lizi's care and Georgia. Lasha softly crossed the yard, stood right before him and asked her:

- Lizi! You're just a same Strong and Winner. So you did find me, didn't you? – Lizi smiled. Get closer to him and held her brother. Suddenly Flora started to look for Max. Three of them started looking for him. The dog wasn't near. Finally they decided to look for him on Charles's cemetery.

They had found a strangest picture there. The dog had brought Charle's inseparable cane to the cemetery... Put it right there under his head and passed away next to him with folded arms just like a human being.